Djinn Bottle Blues

Grimoires Universe

Destiny of a Middle-aged Witch
Book 2

Renee George

Barkside of the Moon Press

Paranormal Mysteries & Romances

By Renee George

Grimoires of a Middle-aged Witch

<u>Grimoires Universe</u>

Peculiar Mysteries & Romances

My Hairy Halloween (Book 4)

In the Midnight Howl (Book 5)

Furred Lines (Book 6)

My Wolfy Wedding (Book 7)

Who Let The Wolves Out? (Book 8)

My Thanksgiving Faux Paw (Book 9)

You Can't Furry Love (Book 10)

Witchin' Impossible Paranormal Mysteries

Witchin' Impossible (Book 1)

Rogue Coven (Book 2)

Familiar Protocol (Booke 3)

Mr & Mrs. Shift (Book 4)

Furred Out (Book 5)

Barkside of the Moon Paranormal Mysteries

Pit Perfect Murder (Book 1)

Murder & The Money Pit (Book 2)

The Pit List Murders (Book 3)

Pit & Miss Murder (Book 4)

The Prune Pit Murder (Book 5)

Two Pits and A Little Murder (Book 6)

Pits and Pieces of Murder (Book 7)

Pittie Party Murder (Book 8)

Nora Black Midlife Psychic Mysteries

Sense & Scent Ability (Book 1)

For Whom the Smell Tolls (Book 2)

War of the Noses (Book 3)

Aroma With A View (Book 4)

Spice and Prejudice (Book 5)

Age of Inno-Scents (Book 6)

Aroma Holiday (Book 7)

The Vapes of Wrath (Book 8)

Hex Drive

Hex Me, Baby, One More Time (Book 1)

Oops, I Hexed It Again (Book 2)

I Want Your Hex (Book 3)

Hex Me With Your Best Shot (Book 4)

Hex Me All Night Long (Book 5)

In my family, danger happens faster than a pixie in heat. I'm Marigold Everlee, a middle-aged eclectic witch with a knack for trouble and a soul that houses a piece of my fiery boyfriend Zev's ifrit spirit.

Talk about a girl on fire. Literally.

Sharing a piece of Zev's soul also gives me access to his fire magic. Oh, yeah, we keep things hot.

After a harrowing rescue mission where I pissed off half the folks in a secret supernatural realm—not to mention a snake goddess who wants Zev all to herself—I knew trouble would find us again.

I just didn't expect it to show up on the same freaking day I brought Zev home. Someone who clearly missed the memo on "leave the people I love alone or get fired from life" has kidnapped my brother Rowan.

What do they want? Zev, of course. My popular fire djinn can't catch a break.

With few options, we enlist the help of Carver, an eclectic witch friend and mentor. Then, we're off to unravel the mystery of Rowan's disappearance. With their help, I'll face this challenge like I do all challenges—head-on.

The kidnappers obviously don't know who they're messing with. And if they harm a hair on my brother's head, I will burn their world to the ground. And stomp on the ashes.

Chapter One

ZEV'S STEADY BREATHING AND THE GENTLE RISE and fall of his chest in the quiet room brought me a peace I hadn't felt in months. How long would he have been trapped in the dark, twisted city of Natheria if I hadn't accidentally spelled a piece of his soul into me? The answer made me shiver. He'd been truly imprisoned, held captive by an immortal monster who would have kept him as her slave forever. But I'd found him with the help of friends, and we freed him.

Natheria was unlike any place I'd ever imagined. A hidden island off the coast of Mexico, cloaked in eternal darkness and populated by creatures most would dismiss as nightmares. Rescuing Zev had been like surviving a fever dream. With the help of Carver, an eccentric witch, and Ryker, a half-djinn tied to the supernatural underworld, we'd faced a demi-god of illusion, a mind-controlling lamia, and storm kelpies intent on drowning us. It was a miracle we'd escaped alive.

It was early Tuesday morning, and we'd been home less than five hours, and I was determined to focus on that victory instead of the creeping dread that lingered in every breath I took. Why was I waiting for the other shoe to drop? Why couldn't I just take the win? I was Marigold Everlee, the epitome of peace, love, and happiness. So why wasn't I jumping for joy?

Because I knew how shattered I'd be if I lost Zev again. I thought I'd loved before, but until the fiery ifrit, I'd never been *in love*.

I shook the stormy thoughts from my mind. There were two things I could count on. The past couldn't be changed, and the future was uncertain. I needed to focus on the present. Zev was back, and whatever challenges awaited us, we'd face them together.

Slipping quietly out of bed, I glanced at the exquisitely handsome djinn one more time. His sun-kissed skin glowed faintly in the dim light, shadows playing across the sharp angles of his jaw. Thick, dark lashes brushed his high cheekbones, framing eyes that, when open, held the molten warmth of amber. His tousled dark hair spilled across the pillow, and even in sleep, his lips curved into a faint smile. Gods, he was breathtaking. It was as if an ancient deity had wandered into the wrong era and ended up in my bed. Hubba hubba. It was impossible to look at him without feeling the magnetic pull of his presence.

He was still recovering, and after our, um, naked aerobic workout, he needed his rest. I watched him for another moment, letting the quiet comfort wash over me, then padded softly into the kitchen.

The explosion from my earlier spell had left black scorch marks on the cabinets, and the acrid scent of burned herbs still clung to the air. That side of the kitchen looked like a battlefield. I grabbed the electric kettle, filled it with water, and set it back on its base.

I tried to push away the swarm of worries buzzing in my head, but no matter how much I focused on the simple task of making tea, the unease gnawed at me.

Iris had found my phone during the ordeal in Mexico. She'd used it to track us to the coast, finding it near the cave where we'd been captured. The battery had almost died, so she'd turned it off. I'd been too distracted, distracted by the extremely hot man, no pun intended, in my bed, to turn it back on.

I plugged it into the charger and powered it up while sitting at the kitchen table, waiting for the kettle to boil. I rubbed the *sebtusiptu* inscription on my palm. It marked me as a vessel for Zev's soul fragment. It was strange having ancient Akkadian script, which looked like pointy triangles, seared into my flesh. Even so, I was grateful. It had been the reason I'd been able to find Zev in the first place.

My phone screen flickered to life, casting the dim room in a soft blue glow. My pulse quickened as notification after notification flooded in. I skimmed through the messages, and with each one, my anxiety deepened.

Iris's texts from before she'd found us popped up first. **Where are you? Why aren't you texting me back? Call me.**

Typical Iris. Impatient, worried, and probably assuming I'd gotten in over my head. She'd been entirely correct, though I'd managed to save myself without my tru-craft sister swooping in. Still, I'd been grateful for the helicopter ride back to Arkansas.

But it was Michael's messages that made my heart skip. **Hey, where do you keep your spell books?** Followed by. **Can't find Uncle Ro. His work called because he didn't show up today.**

4

A knot of anxiety twisted in my gut. Rowan never missed work. Ever.

I scrolled further, freezing when I saw a message from an unknown number. My hands shook as I opened it.

If you want your brother back, meet me in Eureka Springs in two days. Bring only the ifrit, or this won't end well for either of you. I'll text you the location after you arrive.

The words hit me like a physical blow. **Who is this?** I typed frantically. **Prove you have my brother.** My vision blurred as I waited for a reply. The shrill whistle of the kettle felt distant, muffled, like sound underwater. Whoever sent the message wanted me to trade my brother for Zev. My stomach churned. Rowan or Zev. How was I supposed to choose?

My head spun with a flood of conflicting thoughts. Rescuing Zev had come with a steep price, and now Rowan was paying it. The thought made my breath catch as anxiety crept through my veins. I gripped the table's edge, fighting the rising tide of panic.

I grabbed the kettle and poured boiling water into my mug, the steam swirling like a ghostly plume, but I barely noticed the hot liquid as it splashed over the rim. Sharing Zev's soul had made me somewhat heatproof. Still, I checked my skin to see if it was blistering.

Not even red.

I shook my head and refocused on the text. What was I going to do? I refused to lose Rowan. I refused to lose Zev.

The soft creak of the bedroom door jolted me from my spiraling thoughts. I looked over to see Zev standing there, shirtless, his muscles tense as he watched me. Zev crossed the room in quick strides, his presence both comforting and a stark reminder of the impossible choice I was facing.

"I will exchange myself for your brother," Zev said. There was no hesitation, only the calm certainty of someone who had lived long enough to know sacrifices must be made.

I turned sharply to face him. "Are you reading my mind? Can you hear my thoughts now?"

He nodded slowly, his expression softening. "Not all of them," he replied, his voice measured. "But when there are strong emotions behind the thoughts, they come through loud and clear."

I flinched, rubbing the mark on my palm, trying to ease the constant itch that had been there since the symbols first burned into my skin. I couldn't meet his eyes. My voice trembled. "There has to be a better way than handing you over." I hated how weak I sounded.

Zev reached out, gently lifting my chin so that our eyes met. His touch was warm, steady, like the earth itself. "You're not alone, Marigold," he said. "We'll figure it out together."

I exhaled a shaky breath, leaning into his touch. "You're right," I admitted, though my heart twisted painfully. The thought of losing Zev or Rowan was unthinkable.

Zev's eyes narrowed in thought. "The fact that they want me in exchange for Rowan means it's personal. If it weren't for me, you and your brother would be..."

"Stop that." I looked up at him. "But how? Why now? Why my brother? You've made enemies, sure, but this..." My words trailed off. I'd made enemies as well, and very recently. I'd gone to Natheria to find Zev, both barrels blazing, without any thought to the consequences. Was this my payback?

Zev ran a hand through his hair, his brow furrowing as tension settled into his features. "I've angered a lot of people over the years. Some of them very powerful," he said quietly. His gaze wandered toward the window, lost in the faint glow of moonlight. "I've crossed djinn, witches, fae, and even demi-gods at one point or another. And that's just the tip of the mountain. But targeting your brother to get to me? That's inside knowledge that not many would be privy to." He turned and met my gaze, his voice low with anger. "This isn't a random attack. It's an assault on our bond."

"Could it be the Hunter?" I'd beaten the demigod at his own game, and he hadn't been happy about it. And there was another monster I'd pissed off even more. "Or the lamia?" My voice barely carried the name, as the memories of Natheria's cunning, vengeful snake goddess rushed back. She had wanted Zev in the most literal sense, body and soul.

Zev shook his head. "No," he replied firmly. "If it were the lamia, she would have said so in her demands. She would want us to know it was her. That's her way. She thrives on confrontation. This..." His voice trailed off, his eyes narrowing as if piecing together fragments of a puzzle. "This is the work of someone patient, lying in wait for the perfect moment."

I bit my lip, my mind racing. "Do you think it could be another djinn? You said you've crossed some of them before."

Zev hesitated, his eyes distant as old memories resurfaced. "There are a few with the resources," he said carefully. "Almir, the sand djinn, sought my help to bind a rival long ago. I refused him, and he doesn't forgive easily."

"Almir," I repeated, the unfamiliar name sounding strange in my mouth. "Sounds like a real piece of work. But how would he even know about me or Rowan?"

Zev's gaze became distant, his voice taking on an edge, almost mechanical. "Almir keeps spies everywhere. Word of our connection could have reached him. Yet, I doubt this is his doing. Like the lamia, he's more direct in his tactics, as most djinn are." He paused as if weighing his next thought. "There's also Lugh, a trickster wizard once revered as a god of mischief. I bested him in a wager a long time ago. He still carries that loss with him, and the wizard knows how to hold a grudge."

"A trickster god?" The thought of someone whose magic was powerful enough to be worshipped as a god, having Rowan in his grasp, turned my blood to ice. "Could it really be him?"

Zev's eyes darkened, and he crossed his arms. "Lugh delights in chaos," he said slowly. "But I think he would rather play games, pitting us against one another, and not relying on abduction. No, this doesn't feel like his methods."

I shook my head, my frustration growing. "Then who?"

Zev's gaze shifted, a flicker of something darker crossing his face as he leaned forward slightly, his voice dropping lower. "There are others who would seek to harm me. Including a demoness named Karasta." He stroked his short beard. "She's a young demon and far more cunning than some of her older counterparts. We crossed paths a century ago, and I bound her to prevent her from wreaking havoc on a mortal I owed a favor. If she has managed to slip those bonds, she won't hesitate to exact her revenge."

"How did you bind her?"

He gave me a flat stare and said, "My love, this isn't something you want to know."

"Oh?" I blinked as he gave me a meaningful look. "Oh," I said again, but in surprise. He'd seduced the demoness, then bound her. "Cripes."

Hearing him talk about his enemies reminded me that this man had lived for thousands of years before I'd been a twinkle in my bio-dad's eyes, and in the short time I'd known the ifrit, I'd barely scratched the surface of his past. If it wasn't for the urgency of the situation, I would have let sleeping exes lie. After all, I didn't want him looking too hard at my past lovers.

But the situation called for total transparency. "Could she have gotten herself unbound?"

"The binding spell was unbreakable." He

shrugged. "But I hadn't thought anyone could free me from the lamia's control, so...."

I peered at him as I absently stirred my tea. "Does she have a Marigold Everlee in her corner?"

His lips tugged into a sly smile. "She does not."

I smiled back. "Then let's take her off the table for now."

His jaw flexed as he continued to list his enemies. "There's Branvyl, a former member of the Unseelie Court. He's a fae who truly revels in cruelty, and we had quite the clash during the fae wars. I turned down his request for an alliance, and as a result, he lost favor with his queen." He let out a heavy sigh, running his fingers through his messy, thick hair. "I have quite a few enemies, Marigold. What worries me even more is that this kidnapper could be anyone. Even someone I've never met or heard of. I'm not an unknown djinn, and many would gladly use me to gain power or as a bargaining chip with my enemies."

"In other words, we're screwed." I touched his forearm and forced myself to meet his intense gaze. "It's not your fault."

Zev's features softened, and his hand wrapped warmly over mine. "I wish that were true." His tone was gentle. "I'm sorry I've brought this trouble to you and your family."

"Don't talk like that." I forced a pained smile. "Like you said, we'll figure this out. Together."

I'd meant my words to be comforting for both of us, but fear for my brother gnawed relentlessly at my insides. The text had said to bring Zev and no one else, but when it came down to it, we would need help. I thought about asking my sister Iris, then put the thought away. Her magic was amazingly powerful, but it was also unpredictable.

I couldn't count on her staying in the background while I negotiated for Rowan. Besides, if the person who took Rowan knew he was my brother, then surely this same person would know about Iris as well. My mind shifted to Carver. He'd been with us in Natheria, and his understanding of the supernatural ran much deeper than mine. He could be discreet and knew how to navigate this without accidentally getting my brother killed in the process. And he cared for Rowan... perhaps more than he even realized.

I grabbed my phone, my hand trembling. "I should call Carver," I said, my voice stronger and more grounded. "He has spells, contacts, and knowledge that could help us discover who's behind this and get Rowan out of it safely."

Zev nodded, releasing my hand as he leaned back. "Indeed," he agreed. "Carver has been a practitioner of witchcraft long enough to know the ways of the supernatural world. Bringing him in is a good idea."

I was already second-guessing the suggestion. I didn't want to make the wrong call that put Rowan in even more danger. However, there was another scenario I hadn't considered. "We're just assuming the text is true," I told Zev. "We don't even know for sure that Rowan's been taken." I clung to a thin thread of hope. "Maybe he's at home with his phone off. If nothing else, we should call Carver to find out, right?"

Zev raised a brow, the corner of his mouth lifting slightly in quiet acknowledgment of my optimism. "It seems very reasonable," he said, humoring me. "Carver will know if your brother is safe."

I nodded, taking a deep breath. "Okay, I'm calling." I pulled up Carver's contact and hit the call button. My heart raced as the phone rang.

When he answered, his voice was groggy with sleep. "Marigold? What's going on?"

Second-guessing myself again, I hesitated. Was it wise to involve him? Especially if his feelings for Rowan went deeper than friendship.

"Hello?" Carver's voice cut through my thoughts. I heard him chuckle. "Marigold? Are you there, or is this a butt dial?"

Yes, I could trust him. He'd been my rock when we'd gone into Natheria to rescue Zev. I was being silly. I quieted my doubts and steeled my resolve. "I need your help," I told him. "Rowan's been kidnapped."

His voice sharpened immediately. "What? How do you—"

"Is he at the house with you?" I interrupted.

"No," Carver replied. "But... he's at work? He's been doing overnights the last couple of weeks."

I could hear the worry in his tone, so I told him everything. "Michael texted that Rowan hadn't shown up to his job and the hospital called trying to locate him. And then I got a message from an unknown number demanding I bring Zev to Eureka Springs to trade for him."

"Do you have any idea who might have him?" Carver asked, steady but tense.

"Someone who wants Zev," I answered.

"How could they know about Rowan?" Carver pressed.

"It's obvious whoever took him knows that I have a..." I wasn't sure what Zev and I were in concrete terms, so I avoided using a label. "...connection to Zev. It's the only thing that makes sense."

"Or someone from Natheria," Carver said.

"It's a possibility," I agreed.

"I'll be over in a few minutes," Carver said. "We'll make a plan to get him back." He hung up before I could respond.

I set the phone down, feeling numb. Zev wrapped his arms around me, and I leaned into his warmth. "We'll get Rowan back," he whispered, his voice steady. "This I vow to you, my love."

Hearing him call me his love eased the knot in my chest. I nodded, appreciating the determination in his voice. "I hope telling Carver was the right decision."

Zev pulled back slightly, meeting my gaze. He squeezed my hand. "It was the right call," he said, his words firm.

"Maybe," I muttered, then straightened, meeting his determination with my own. "But let me make one thing crystal clear... I'm not losing either of you. Not Rowan. Not you. We'll find another way."

Zev's eyes gleamed with quiet pride, and he pulled me into his arms again. "With Marigold Everlee in our corner, I would expect nothing less."

Chapter Two

It took less than ten minutes for Carver to arrive at my house. He looked disheveled but alert, his dark eyes filled with worry. The early June morning was chilly, but since the spell that soulbonded us, I'd noticed I didn't get easily cold. Or maybe it was perimenopause. Either way, I was glad for the cooler temperatures.

I hugged him. "You must've run every stop sign in town."

"It's the middle of the night, and there's no traffic." He gave me a quick squeeze back, let go, and got right down to business. "What's the plan?"

"The message said we needed to be in Eureka Springs in two days," I told him. "The kidnapper is supposed to give us more instructions after we arrive."

"Two days?" Carver asked. "When was the text sent?"

My gut knotted. I hadn't paid attention to the time and date stamp. We'd spent two days traveling to Mexico and back. I grabbed my phone from the table and opened my messages. Crap. "It was sent around twelve hours hours ago."

"This changes nothing," Zev replied flatly. "Whether it's two days or one, we will get your brother back. As I said before, I'll exchange myself for him."

"The hell you will," I snapped before I could stop myself. "I mean..."

"Where life exists, there is hope, libbu sa."

I rolled my eyes. "If you call what was happening to you in Natheria life, then...okay," I said blandly.

"Zev's right," Carver jumped in. "We have to do everything we can to protect Rowan."

I whipped my gaze to the lanky witch. "You don't think I know that? He's my brother. Of course, we have to protect him, but I can't trade one life for another." Unless it's my own, I thought. I would trade places with him in a heartbeat. I just needed to figure out a way for the kidnappers to want me more than an ifrit. Maybe my connection to Zev, the fact that I had a piece of his soul inside me, could push the needle.

Zev's expression soured. "I would destroy myself before I allowed you to take my place."

I forgot that he could read my thoughts. Ugh. "No more talk of self-destruction, got it?"

He gave me a tight smile. "Whoever it is will not be able to destroy me. Rowan isn't immortal."

I narrowed my gaze at him. "They can trap you," I countered. "Forever."

A million things that I wanted to say played out in my head. My mind was utter chaos. How dare Zev act as if his life was less important than mine? How dare Carver act like I'd prioritize a man over my brother? As if I would allow my hormones to make crucial decisions. Gah. Men. Instead, I rolled my eyes. "How about we all take a breath?" I needed to calm down, possibly more than they did.

"Time is running out," Carver said as if we all weren't aware of the time constraint.

I pulled up maps on my phone screen and typed in Eureka Springs. "It'll take us one hour and eighteen minutes to get there." The message had been sent a little over twelve hours ago, so we had until tomorrow to figure our shit out. The text doesn't give us a specific time for when we need to arrive in Eureka Springs." Something else dawned on me. "When this message was sent, we were still trying to find and free

Zev. This means Rowan's kidnapping can't be about Lamia or Hunter." I shook my head. "We hadn't pissed either of them off when the text was sent." This also meant... "You've been gone for seven months. Whoever this is had to have been aware of our short-lived relationship but didn't know you ghosted me."

Zev frowned. "I didn't ghost you. I was captured."

"Potatoes, poh-tah-toes." I pished him. "The point is, it can't be someone from Natheria."

Carver raised his hand.

I rolled my eyes. "You don't have to raise your hand to talk."

"Okay, Professor." He pursed his lips. "You're not taking into account that the person who has Rowan might be a seer or has hired a seer to know where Zev would be, who he would be with, and when he would be there. They could've waited months or years for the opportunity to capture Zev at his most vulnerable." He gave me a meaningful look. "The fact that he's missing a piece of soul could be why this is happening now."

Was he intimating this was my fault? My shit was so close to being lost. I bristled at the idea but didn't argue. I could only deal with the parts of this conversation that would benefit our current situation. Taking a deep breath, I focused on the now. "So seers are real?"

Both Carver and Zev simultaneously said, "Yes."

I wasn't surprised that fortune tellers existed, not after everything I'd seen since finding out my sister Iris was a tru-craft witch. Still...freaking seers existed? Wild. "We still agree, though, that this is most likely someone from Zev's past. I mean, taking my brother feels really personal."

"Likely," Zev agreed. "This is why I shouldn't have involved you in my life, Marigold. My world is dangerous. Too dangerous for mortals."

He could screw off with all that noise. "I'm not a fainting goat who topples over at the first sign of trouble."

"No." He shook his head, the fire in his eyes flaring to life. "You are like a bull who runs headfirst at every red flag."

I whipped my gaze at the irritating ifrit. Even if what he said was true, hearing it from his lips pissed me the hell off.

"Marigold," he said softly, his irises turning a dark citrine.

"What?" I snapped.

"You're on fire."

I glanced down, my eyes widening as flames danced along my bare arms. I waved my arms around to get rid of them. Luckily, the fire died before damaging me or my already explosified kitchen.

"It's nothing," I said quickly, knowing it was likely a side effect of the spell that put Zev's soul fragment inside me. "You know I've had some fire magic since the spell." I'd had several moments when I'd been in danger in Natheria where the ability to call fire had come in handy. "But it's not our first priority." I narrowed my gaze on Zev. "No more talk of bulls and red flags, okay?"

Zev grunted a half-hearted agreement.

"Back to the problem at hand then," Carver said, glancing between Zev and me, his expression worried. "If this is about settling a score with you..." He nodded to Zev. "...then we need to know every possible player."

"Impossible, my friend." Zev crossed his arms, leaning against the wall, his expression thoughtful. "We've already discussed it, and the list is as long as my existence, and Rowan doesn't have the time for us to narrow it down sufficiently."

Carver's hands balled into fists. "Then we should go now. We can scout the town and see if we can get any information on whoever is behind this."

We couldn't just show up in Eureka Springs a day early. The danger for my brother was too high. "One problem." I raised a finger. "The person or

21

people who have Rowan will recognize us if we just show up willy-nilly, and you weren't invited to the party."

Carver nodded emphatically, his dark hair falling over his eyes as he began to pace. "I have something that can help in that department," he countered. "Have you ever heard of poly-juice potion?"

Zev shook his head. "That's not a magic I'm familiar with."

I gave the fire djinn an incredulous look. "I can't believe you've never watched Harry Potter."

He shrugged. "Is that a movie? I don't watch movies or television. I prefer reading."

I arched a brow at him. "What kind of books?"

"My tastes are varied. I like a good urban fantasy but will also read the occasional historical romance, biography, and even a few cozy mysteries."

His sexiness was already a ten on a scale of one to ten, but the reading comment took him to a twenty.

"If we don't have time to go through Zev's enemies, we certainly don't have time to go through his list of favorite books," Carver said tersely, stopping his pacing. "I have the recipe for a transformation potion that can alter our appearances." He tugged his lower lip between his teeth before letting it go. Tentatively, he added, "There are some...side effects, though."

I frowned. "Like what?"

"Nothing too terrible." He shrugged a little too nonchalantly, which told me the side effects were going to be pretty awful.

I rolled my hand to hurry him along. "Spit it out."

He nodded. "A complete loss of smell and the ability to see in color."

"No scents, and the whole world will be black and white," I reiterated.

"More grayscale," Carver said, "but yes. You won't see colors while on the potion. It seems to deactivate olfactory receptor neurons and the cones in the retina."

I thought about it for a moment. "That doesn't seem all that bad. I mean, I thought you were going to say that we'd grow boils on our asses."

"Uhm, yeah, boils." Carver shuffled his feet nervously. "No worries there."

"How long does it last?" Zev asked.

"When the transformation ends, your senses return to normal," Carver replied.

I was terrible with numbers, but even I knew the math wasn't mathing. "That's pretty non-specific timewise. Try that answer again, but in minutes and hours."

Carver sucked his teeth, then added, "The spell will last twelve to twenty-four hours..."

He was still holding back. Why? "And...."

His eyes pivoted to the floor momentarily before lifting to meet my gaze. "And you can't reverse the spell once it takes effect. You just have to let it run its course."

Now I understood his hesitation. The potion's fluctuating timeline could be a big freaking problem. "In other words, we'd have to wait for it to wear off before we make a show of arriving in Eureka Springs."

He shrugged. "It's still dark out. If we take the potion soon, it will be over before the sun comes up tomorrow."

I chewed the inside of my cheek for a moment as I considered the plan. Honestly, there wasn't a single scenario that I could come up with that was any better than the eclectic witch's idea. I glanced at Zev.

He inclined his head in the affirmative.

Turning back to Carver, I told him, "Let's do it."

On my agreement, his eyes lit up with excitement.

Until he looked at my kitchen stove.

"We're going to have to cook the potion base at

Rowan's. My ingredients are there, and he has a working kitchen."

"Good." I nodded. "It will give me a chance to look around."

"I didn't see any signs of a break-in or struggle," Carver said. "And believe me, I looked."

"You were there for seconds before you sped across town to get here," I told him. His shoulders sagged, and I put a comforting hand on his arm. "Some extra eyes to investigate while you cook won't hurt a thing, and who knows, maybe we'll find something that will clue us in on whose ass we need to kick."

He gave me a sideways glance as his worried frown turned into a worried half-smile. "You're right."

"I know." I gave him a smile back and squeezed his shoulder. "But it's always nice to hear."

"We should go soon," Zev said, breaking the brief kumbaya moment.

"Give me two minutes," I told them. "I need to pack a few things before we go." Like my cell phone charger, a portable battery, a few toiletries, and a change of clothes. I needed a full battery just in case the kidnappers texted again.

"I'll head over now." Carver rattled his keys. "I

can get started on the base while you two get whatever you need to get."

"See you soon." I gave him another quick hug. "We'll get him back," I whispered fiercely into his ear.

Carver leaned back, his dark eyes brimming with concern. "We have to."

And he was right. There was no other choice. Rowan was an innocent caught in a snare of bullshit because he was related to me. Getting him home and in one piece was the only option, and I would see it done.

As Carver left, Zev's hand slipped into my palm, his fingers lacing mine. "*We* will see it done," he corrected me, reminding me once again that I wasn't alone. This wasn't just my problem to solve. I had backup who would move heaven and earth to help me get my brother back.

I gave Zev a grateful smile and nodded. "We."

Chapter Three

Rowan's house loomed ahead. The three-story Victorian stood out on the quiet street full of traditional stone cottages and neoclassical prairie homes. The Victorian was painted pale yellow, and the trim around the windows and the wrap-around porch were a rich burgundy. He'd bought the place at an estate auction fifteen years ago as a fixer-upper and had taken great care in restoring it to its former glory. Every detail whispered that someone meticulous lived there, someone with taste and an eye for authenticity. It described my brother to a tee.

Since starting our eclectic witch journey with Carver, Rowan had been coming to my house two to three times a week for lessons. The one and only time I suggested we do it at his place, he put the kibosh on the idea with prejudice.

"You're messy, Mare," he'd said to me. "And that's without magic. I don't need you blowing up any of my furniture." I'd scoffed and told him he was being ridiculous, but my kitchen was proof positive my bro was nobody's fool.

I got out of the car before Zev and headed up the sidewalk. I left my overnight bag in the backseat but took my purse with me. My stomach ached as I approached the large wraparound porch. The knot of fear that had formed in my stomach when I saw the terrible text message felt even tighter as we stepped onto the porch. Rowan was in the hands of someone who might harm him, and it was my fault. My messy choices had brought danger to my family's door. If anything happened to my brother, I'd never forgive myself.

I felt Zev's hand low on my back. "It's not your fault."

I hopped up the last step to put some distance between us. I didn't deserve comfort, not from Zev or anyone, and in the moment, his efforts only made me feel worse. "Stop reading my mind," I grumbled, unable to keep the irritation from my voice.

His hand fell away. "I will try, *libbu sa*."

"Come in," Carver said as he opened the door for us. He was holding a steaming mug of something pungent that didn't smell like coffee or cocoa.

I wrinkled my nose. "Is the potion done?"

"Almost." He shook his head. "I've cooked the base and gathered the ingredients, but I still have to put them together." His fingers, cupping the mug, trembled slightly as he ushered us inside. He had been staying at Rowan's for the past seven months. I hadn't thought much of it at first. Carver once told me that he had always been a bit nomadic, crashing at friends' places between magical jobs or when inspiration struck him to hole up somewhere for days on end. Seeing the strain on his face and the tension in his movements, I knew without a doubt Rowan wasn't a fleeting fancy for him.

My brother's living room featured two burgundy leather armchairs, a sable blue velvet loveseat, and tasteful art pieces curated by Rowan over the years. The polished wood floors gleamed under soft lighting, and a grand staircase swept upward to the second floor, with a dark, polished oak banister.

Nothing seemed out of place. That disturbed me the most.

Zev's amber eyes flickered with fire as we crossed the room, unreadable but alert. I could sense his growing frustration simmering beneath the surface. He still wasn't up to full power. Before his imprisonment by Lamia, he could've changed his appearance at will and wouldn't have needed a transformation spell. He could still call his fire and control the magic of his flames, but his other magic took more power than he had to give. Another thing that felt like my fault. If I hadn't cast the spell that put his soul inside me...

His low growl silenced my intrusive thoughts. "I'll search upstairs for signs of Rowan's abductors," he said before splitting off from us and going up the steps to the second floor.

I ran my fingers along the edge of a side table as if expecting to find a trace of anything that would explain what happened to my brother. But everything was in order.

"I couldn't find any clues to his kidnapping," Carver groused, his voice thick with frustration. "Come on. I'll need yours and Zev's blood to finish your part of the potion."

When he headed toward the stairs, I furrowed my brow. "Where are we going?"

"My room," he replied.

"Not the kitchen?"

"The rest of the potion doesn't require cooking, and my supplies are in my room along with my spell-crafting altar." He shook his head. "It's easier to finish up there than to haul everything, including the altar, downstairs."

"Gotcha." I nodded. "Makes sense."

Still, for some reason, I was reluctant to go up. Was I avoiding Zev? I'd spent so long waiting and wondering, and now that I had him back, it seemed like everything was going to shit. Having these thoughts would usually be okay. I was used to being a jumbled mess of inner conflict, but the fact that Zev could read my mind made the situation doubly difficult.

While I could control my actions, I couldn't control all the racing thoughts, the feeling of doom, or the impulsive ideas mucking with my head. I had ADHD, and this was how my brain worked. After a lifetime of living with it, I'd learned to control the things I said out loud...for the most part...but I couldn't stop my inner dialogue from having diarrhea of the mouth. I loved Zev, but if he kept reading my mind, there was no guarantee he would keep loving me.

Even so, I wouldn't let fear hold me back. So, I did what I always did in these situations. I sucked it up, put my big girl panties on, and followed Carver to the second floor.

The master bedroom door was open and the room was immaculate, other than his unmade bed. Had they snatched him while he was sleeping?

Zev shook his head as he moved silently through the room, his gaze sharp, inspecting every detail. His bare arms were tense, muscles coiled beneath his skin like a lion waiting to pounce. "There's no sign of struggle," he murmured, his voice low and controlled. "Whoever took him did it cleanly."

"I know," Carver said. "I've hit the room with a discovery spell, and it gave me nothing."

I swallowed hard. "We'll find him. I swear to you." I wasn't sure who I was trying to convince more, Carver or myself.

"Whatever it takes," Zev added. He gave a curt nod and moved to the bay window, peering out into the street. "The sun will rise soon. We have to be quick. Time isn't on our side."

Carver led the way to the guest room where he'd been staying. The door creaked as he pushed it open, revealing a far more chaotic space than the rest of Rowan's house. Books, spell components, and old texts were scattered across a large dresser and the floor, and his black leather witch's bag was open on his bed.

His spell-crafting altar stood beneath an east-facing window. "I do a lot of ˙spells that require natural light," he explained as he set down his mug and arranged herbs, vials of crushed crystals, and essential oils onto the rectangular table. The tabletop was hardwood with alchemy symbols burned into the surface. At the center was a large selenite plate he used to cleanse and charge his tools, stones, and crystals, but he'd also taught us that selenite could be used to amplify spellwork to create more potent and effective potions and talismans.

I watched Carver handle each item carefully, placing them around the plate, before putting three small beakers on the selenite. His meticulousness was mesmerizing. He used a dropper to extract the potion base from the mug and add the murky substance to the glass beakers.

"I'll need these," he muttered, more to himself than to me, as he finished the layout. "Bloodstone, lavender, and something for the stabilizer…" He trailed off as he grabbed a small silver knife from a side pocket of his bag and set it next to the bloodstone. "This will do it." He deftly combined herbs, crushed crystals, and oil into a mortar bowl.

"This will work on Zev, too, right?" I asked as he began combining the ingredients by crushing them with the pestle. "He's not exactly human. Will it work on ifrits?"

"None of us in this room are exactly human," Carver said. He gave me a half smile and a slight head shake. "Don't worry. Each potion will be matched to our individual blood." Carver didn't look up from his task as he continued. "It'll hold. It's not perfect, but it'll do." Before I could ask more, he held up a finger and said, "Give me a minute. I have to pray to Hecate while I finish the blending, and I need to concentrate while I do it."

"Heard," I told him. "I'll busy myself elsewhere until you're ready."

I took the opportunity to check out Rowan's home office. It was the smallest of the three upstairs bedrooms and down at the end of the hall. The door opened with a slight creak. Rowan's desk was tucked against the wall in front of a picture window, neat and organized as always. At the center of his desktop, against the wall, was what looked like a decorative wooden storage box with a design made of geometric shapes inlaid into the surface with darker wood that reminded me of two swans facing each other. The edges were dull with patina, marking it an antique. I hadn't remembered seeing it there before. I picked it up and realized it didn't even have a lid. Maybe Rowan had just liked the way it looked. My brother was like that with his antiques.

I set it back down then opened every drawer in Rowan's desk, half-expecting to find something that would explain all this, some note, anything that might tell us what had happened. But there was nothing out of the ordinary. Nothing but a few pens and a neatly stacked pile of documents. I opened the rest of the drawers, and, again, nothing out of the ordinary.

Damn it. Still, something about the room felt wrong, as if something was missing. I thought about when I'd been in Rowan's office with him. He would sometimes dictate patient notes at home, so he kept an old-fashioned recorder in his desk for those occasions. I'd teased him about using a recorder and not his smartphone. I'd accused him of being stuck in the dark ages. But Rowan had told me that there were too many ways that patients' data could be stolen if it was connected to an unsecured internet connection or even via Bluetooth. With all the data breaches in the news over the past few years, it had been hard to argue with his logic.

So where was the recorder now? He would've brought it home from work, so it should be somewhere around here.

I opened every drawer again, running my finger inside each one, my heart sinking as I came up with nothing.

"Hey!" Carver's raised voice cut through my curiosity. "Come back. I'm ready."

I hurried back to Carver's bedroom. The sooner we got this done, the sooner we could get on the road.

The thin-framed witch nodded to three beakers. "The potion will change our appearances for at least twelve hours," he said. "Its side effects won't be comfortable, but they won't hurt, and the spell will hold."

That might have been the third or fourth time he'd said the spell would hold. The fact that he kept repeating it like a mantra worried me.

He used an alchemical ladle, a silver instrument with a tiny spoon tip and long handle, to place several small scoops of the herb-crystal-oil mixture into the three glasses. The liquid base inside them began to shimmer, taking on a strange, iridescent hue. After, he picked up the silver athame. "I need your blood for this next part," he said.

I stuck my hand out. "Do it."

I winced as the pointed end of the blade pierced the pad of my thumb. Carver dropped the knife into a cup of clear liquid off to the side of the selenite plate, then, with both hands, held my thumb over one of the small beakers and squeezed a few drops of my blood into the swirling mixture. The iridescent potion turned green.

"Is it supposed to turn that color?"

He nodded. "Yes."

He took the blade out of the cup and then wiped it with a clean cloth.

"What's in there?"

"Sanitizer." He gave me a patient smile, one that I'd seen him wear during our many lessons over the past few months. "We don't want our blood mixing into each other's potions."

"Why not?"

"We need the potion to identify your DNA so that it can be changed. If Zev's or my blood were mixed in, the results would be...unpredictable." He shook his head. "And I don't want to find out just how unpredictable."

"Roger that."

He poked Zev's thumb next. The potion turned black.

My eyes widened.

Carver said, "It's okay. Zev's an ifrit. It's going to look different."

When Carver's solution turned blue, I started having doubts that my eclectic witch friend knew what the hell he was doing. But I was desperate, and desperate times called for desperate potions.

"What now?"

"Now we add the not-so-secret ingredient," he said, opening a pouch with forty vials of something dark lining the inside. "Pick your poison."

I jerked my chin. "It's poison?"

"Don't be so literal, Marigold. It's blood."

I wasn't sure that was better. "From who?"

"Willing donors," he assured me. "The blood will bind the originator's appearance to the spell."

It still didn't sound better. "So we're drinking other people's blood. Like vampires."

"Not like vampires, but I won't sugarcoat it. This is blood magic. It's dangerous and unpredictable."

"Dangerous and unpredictable," I said, my tone slightly strangled. "My middle names."

Zev covered a chuckle.

"The blood was from willing human donors, and the spell pulls from the essence of the donated blood, not the person themself. You won't find yourself developing any strange habits or traits."

"Got it." I gave him a playful grin. "So, no sudden cravings for, I don't know, blood, or turning into a werewolf at the full moon?"

"No. You'll be just fine." Carver shot me a dry look. "Do you have a preference for your appearance?"

"You pick for me," I told Carver. "Just don't make me hideous."

Zev nodded. "You can pick for me as well, my friend. I don't care if I'm hideous."

I put my hand on Carver's. "Don't make him hideous either."

That bought me a genuine smile from the eclectic witch. "There's not an ugly donor in the bunch."

"Fantastic. Let's do it." I knew we didn't have any more time to waste. "Draw me like one of your French girls."

Chapter Four

CARVER TOOK THE BLOOD SAMPLES, POURING A different one into each beaker and giving them a stir. He handed one to each of us. I held mine up to the light, watching the green liquid swirl inside the glass.

"Once you drink this, the change will be almost immediate," Carver explained. "We won't look like ourselves, but more importantly, no one outside of this room will know it's us."

I glanced at Zev, who nodded slightly. Then, without further hesitation, I tossed the potion back like it was happy hour on Ladies' Night. The liquid was cool as it slid down my throat, leaving a faint metallic taste in my mouth. Almost instantly, I felt a strange sensation, like my skin was shifting, my bones reshaping and shortening beneath the surface.

"Okay," I said, holding out my shrinking hands. "This is getting super weird."

Zev followed suit, his expression impassive as he downed the potion, though I could see the flicker of discomfort in his eyes as the magic took hold.

Carver was the last to drink, his gaze lingering on the empty vial for a moment before he set it aside. "It's done."

Looking at Zev was like looking at a stranger. His chestnut hair, soft and warm, fell over his forehead, making him look almost boyish. The soft brown tones contrasted sharply with his usual dark hair. His thin, delicate face featured startling blue eyes that resembled a clear autumn sky. As I studied him, I realized it didn't matter what face he wore, how he held himself, and his intense gaze told me he was still my ifrit.

Carver had become a muscular redhead with a smattering of freckles. His coloring reminded me of Rowan, and I'd wondered if he'd chosen that appearance on purpose.

"How do I look?" I asked.

Zev raised a brow. "Different."

I frowned. "Different good or different bad?"

He didn't answer. Instead, he said, "Go look for yourself."

"Okaaaaay." I shot a look at Carver. "You didn't give me a third nostril, did you?"

He chuckled, but didn't answer.

Not good.

I hurried to the mirror hanging behind Carver's dresser, grabbing my skirt before it could fall off new, slender hips. My boots were loose and slapped the floor like clown shoes. I glanced at my reflection and didn't recognize the woman staring back at me. My peasant blouse was more like a sack dress, because I was much shorter, thinner, almost as thin as our friend Ryker. My features were softer, younger, and unfamiliar. I had long, golden blond hair that spilled over my shoulders and bright blue eyes. My skin felt different, too, as it stretched over unfamiliar bones.

"Sorry, Mare. I didn't think about how your clothes would fit when I picked Nikky's blood."

"Nikky?"

"A friend," he said. "I could probably find a pair of sweats with a drawstring, and Rowan has smaller feet than the two of us. He has some tennis shoes that might work. They still might be a bit big on you, but at least they'd be smaller than your boots.

My blouse hit me just above my knees, so I dropped my skirt and asked Carver, "Do you have a belt?"

He went to his closet and grabbed a black woven belt with a silver buckle. "Will this work?"

I cinched it around my waist then stood back and admired my handiwork. "Interesting," I muttered, running a hand through my new hair. I smiled a perky little smile and wiggled my skinny hips. "Not bad at all."

"I prefer tall, dark-haired beauties with a few curves," Zev said.

"Good answer." I rewarded him with a smile. I looked at my left palm. It no longer had that slight itch, and the triangles were gone. I turned my attention to Carver. "So, this isn't just an illusion spell, right? We have been physically transformed."

Carver nodded. "Not an illusion," he explained. "Illusions are too easy to see through, especially for those in the supernatural world. They'd pick up on the discrepancies, the way shadows don't align, the faint aura of magic clinging to us. No, we're fully transformed at the cellular level. The change is real."

"So, I'm a real blonde, now, huh?" I smirked. "I never thought I'd say that."

Carver shrugged, amusement playing at the corners of his mouth. "I thought you could pull it off. And besides, they say blondes have more fun, right?"

"I've always wondered about that." I snorted, shaking my head. "Time to find out."

"Let's go," Zev said. "The sooner we get to Eureka Springs, the better."

He was right, of course. We didn't know who had taken Rowan or their full intentions, but it was clear that time was ticking on our spell and Rowan. Every moment spent here was a moment closer to something we couldn't control.

"I'm ready," Carver said, closing up his leather bag and slinging it over his shoulder. "We have a lot of ground to cover once we reach our destination."

I nodded, still marveling at the change in my appearance. The blonde hair, the lighter eyes—it wasn't me. Carver had said there were side effects, but so far, other than the change in my appearance, I felt fine. "I thought we were going to lose our ability to see color and smell stuff."

"It will happen," he said. "The one time I used this potion, it kicked in at around twenty minutes."

"Fun," I said flatly. "Something to look forward to."

As we prepared to leave Rowan's house, I asked, "Did you see Rowan's dictation recorder anywhere?"

Carver shook his head. "It should be in his desk."

"It's not," I told him.

He frowned. "That's odd."

"That's what I thought."

I had considered all the ways the recorder could

be helpful or unhelpful, and it took me two seconds to decide it was important enough to give it more thought. "Do you have a location spell or something to help me find it?"

Carver chewed the inside of his lip for a moment, then shook his head. "No, but if Rowan wanted to keep it from whoever took him, I might know where he hid it."

We followed him down the hall to Rowan's office.

"It's not in here," I said. "I searched every drawer."

Carver didn't respond. He walked over to the desk and touched the decorative wooden box with the palm of his hand. I heard a click and a snap as the top lifted and shifted sideways.

"It's a magic puzzle box," I whispered.

"Only mine or Rowan's hand can open it," Carver confirmed. "It was...a gift."

Inside the box were some ticket stubs, a yellow ribbon, and some folded paper, and holding it all down was the Dark Ages dictation recorder.

"That's it," I said excitedly. Although, I don't know what I hoped to hear. Most likely, it would be a note about some patient who'd come into the emergency room with the flu than anything important, but still...

Carver retrieved the recorder, rewound it thirty seconds, and pushed the play button.

We heard Rowan, mid-sentence, say, "*...patient had a three-inch laceration on his—*"

"*Gabeta en druthan!*" a voice sounded as if shouted in the distance.

"*Carver?*" Rowan asked.

The intruder, his voice louder and closer, said, "*Naton destutu mi, druidacos se tonaros.*"

"*Shit,*" my brother hissed into the recorder. "*They're upstairs.*" He must have grabbed his cell phone because he swore again and said, "*Why are there no bars?*" We could hear a rustle of blinds. He spoke quickly. "*There's a white SUV parked out front. Hard to make out the model from this angle. A tall man with silver or white hair, it's hard to tell with the gas streetlights. His hair is long and pulled up into a top knot. I don't know if he is with the people in the house, but it's Sunday, ten at night, so I'm guessing he is.*"

A loud pounding on the door made my heart race. "*Gamaros uetonos, Doktoros Everlee, agus non se denkas. Cumascertos, Mapos Taranou, agus bidis ulamuros,*" the man roared. Then a guttural voice spoke in English. "*Surrender, and you won't be harmed, Doktoros Everlee. Resist, and you will wish for death.*"

"*I don't know who they are or why they're here. Maybe something to do with Iris, but it's not good,*" Rowan whispered rapidly. "*Carver, I... I hope you're safe, and I hope you return and find this recording. I don't know what's going to happen but...*"

The banging on Rowan's door became violently loud.

"*Okay, okay,*" my brother shouted. "*I surrender.*" Then, quietly, he added, "*Find me.*"

The recording ended.

Carver had paled. "He left this message for me."

"What was the weird language?" I asked.

"It sounds like a form of Gaulish," Zev said.

"Isn't that a dead language?" I knew from ancient history classes that Gaul had encompassed a massive portion of Western Europe, now occupied by modern-day France, Belgium, the Netherlands, Germany, and Italy.

Zev nodded. "It hasn't been around for more than two thousand years. Not since the Roman Empire conquered the area."

"Can you translate what was said?" Carver inquired eagerly.

Zev's eyes darkened with frustration. "I only picked up a few words here or there, but it's been a very long time. I recognize the sounds and cadence, but that's about it." He paused for a moment as if considering something, then added, "I might know someone who can help."

"Call your friend on the move," Carver said, slinging the black leather bag with all his spell ingredients over his shoulder. "Maybe something the kidnapper said will give us more information on why and where they took Ro."

Knowing Rowan was taken by strangers who spoke in a language no modern society had spoken in two thousand-plus years made me feel sick to my stomach. *Surrender, and you won't be harmed, Doktoros Everlee, resist, and you will wish for death.* I hoped the kidnapper had meant it, when he said Rowan wouldn't be harmed. I had to hold on to the hope because the alternative would drive me mad.

Zev called his contact, but there was no answer. He left a text for the person to call him back. When Carver was ready, we loaded into my car and got on the road.

We would find Rowan. We had to.

I glanced again at the blue-eyed Goldie Locks staring back at me in the rearview mirror and tried to force my doubts away. And if anyone stood in our way, well...they were about to learn that blondes weren't just for fun—this undercover brunette was downright dangerous.

Chapter Five

I DROVE BECAUSE ZEV DIDN'T LIKE DRIVING. As a
djinn, most of his traveling had been by magical
means, and Carver was in the back seat, earbuds in,
mixing a few spells we might need once we got to
Eureka Springs and listening to the dictation
recording over and over. I'd gotten so used to being
over six feet tall since the goddess Macha had turned
me into a half-giantess, so I'd had to adjust the seat
forward and up several inches to accommodate my
new height of five feet two inches. Even before
becoming super tall, I'd been over five-foot-eight.
Being this tiny felt all kinds of wrong.

During the first ten minutes of the drive, we
discussed our plan of action. As it turned out, we
didn't have much of one. Carver had put on an

enchanted ring that vibrated near active magic, but since the three of us were under transformation spells, the damn thing hadn't stopped buzzing. Zev said he could see auras, but the side effects of the spell had kicked in for him, and he couldn't distinguish colors. That did us about as much good as Carver's magic bullet finger. Eventually, the three of us settled on a "go in, poke around, and see what we see" strategy.

Needless to say, I wasn't feeling great about our chances. "My dad used to say, 'having a bad plan is worse than no plan.'"

"Do you have a better idea?" Carver asked.

"Nope," I told him. I cast a sideways glance at Zev. Some days, he seemed so modern that it was hard to believe he'd been alive for thousands of years. The fact that he had known ancient societies who spoke dead languages was fantastical. If these ancient dead language speakers hadn't kidnapped my brother, I might have even called it wonderful. "What can you tell us about the Gauls?" I asked him. "Do they even still exist?"

"Most of the Gauls were integrated into the Roman Empire," Zev replied.

He still hadn't gotten a response from his contact. It was early in the morning, and it hadn't been that long, so I was practicing something I wasn't very good at... *patience.*

"I looked them up," Carver said from the back. "The Gauls had limited writings, which made their language difficult to study. I couldn't get any traction on any of the words we heard, except *doktoros,* which I assume means doctor. Zev, what kind of dealings did you have with them?"

"Not much. Not directly." My man's brows furrowed. "They were proud warriors, but they lacked strategic thinking. Their leader angered the wrong person with his demands."

"The wrong person?" I asked curiously.

"Julius Caesar," Zev answered.

"The Julius Caesar? You knew him?" I resisted the urge to say, *Et tu, Brute?* While it was entirely inappropriate, it took all my willpower to hold back.

"Yes. I was traded to him by my old master in a bargain that would free us both in 58 B.C., right as the Gallic Wars began. The man had used me to gain an advantage over the Helvetii by discovering and relaying their escape routes to his army, and in the end, Caesar's forces defeated them."

"How badly?" I asked.

"Scorched earth would be an appropriate description," he replied sourly.

Through our bond, I could sense that the memory still disturbed him. "It's not your fault," I told him. "You were trapped by a djinn bargain."

"One of my own making," he said, almost too quietly to hear. "I wanted my freedom, and it only cost the blood of hundreds of thousands of men, women, and children."

I stifled a gasp. That was a huge burden for anyone to bear. How did Zev live with the horror?

He looked out the window and said, "When you're immortal, living with your past sins is inevitable."

I didn't scold him for reading my thoughts. The ache of his pain was enough to hold my tongue.

It was Carver who spoke up. "Unless you murdered them yourself, you aren't to blame. Caesar was a tyrant who would have conquered Gaul and the Helvetii with or without your help. He saw himself as an empire builder and would stop at nothing to see his vision for power and glory manifest. You're not responsible for the terrible things he did to achieve his goals."

Zev didn't respond, but I could feel his turmoil uncoil a little. I glanced in the rearview mirror and met Carver's gaze before giving him a small grateful nod.

"Do you think any of them could have made a deal with some magical being to get revenge on you for helping the Romans?"

Zev shook his head. "They never knew who or what I was. I was a scout for the Roman commander. Nothing more."

"After, did Caesar give you your freedom?"

"Not right away." His gaze narrowed. "After stirring discontent in his senate, I made certain his knowledge of me died with him."

I couldn't hold it back any longer. "*Et tu, Brute?*"

Zev rolled his eyes and grinned. "Feel better?"

"Yes," I said frankly. I taught women's studies at Darling University, so I knew a little about strong women in history. "During the Gallic Wars, Gaul women would shout at their men during battles, reminding them why they had to win. And if their men were killed in combat, then the women would kill their children and themselves to avoid becoming slaves to the Romans."

"Talk about incentive," Carver said.

"Yes," Zev confirmed. "The women of Gaul were as fierce as the men. Some of them were warriors who fought alongside their men. But the Romans were highly trained soldiers. In the end, the Gauls were killed or enslaved."

Carver had his phone out, and I could see the screen glowing in the rearview mirror. "Caesar wrote in a book that the Romans killed over a million Gauls, yet hardly any of his men died."

Zev shook his head and scoffed. "Victors write the history books. Many Gauls died during the Gallic Wars, but the Romans did not come out of it unscathed. Thousands of soldiers were killed in combat."

I sniffed. "Is it bad that I'm happy Caesar was stabbed a gazillion times by his own senate?"

It was at that moment the potion's side effects kicked in, and I lost my sense of smell and the ability to see colors. I pumped the brakes in response and slowed down as Highway 62 East turned into an inky ribbon that wound through the monochrome Ozark mountains. The sky had lightened on the horizon, our only indication that dawn was near. Being unable to see color had turned my world into an old black-and-white movie.

I kind of hated it. I never realized just how much I relied on color for identification as well as beauty.

"Are you okay?" Zev asked.

"Gentleman and gentleman," I announced. "We have achieved fifty shades of gray, and not in a sexy way." A shadow in the road that looked like an animal caused me to swerve. "This is going to get old real quick."

There was no direct route from Southill Village, so I'd taken 62 all the way to the southern edge of town and turned north on Highway 23-South Main Street. The town was awash with Victorian architecture, their spires and dormer windows catching the early morning sunrise and casting eerie shadows across the pebbly-looking cobblestone streets.

I shivered as the lack of color made me feel like we were entering a gothic horror. Carver had booked two suites at the 1905 Basin Park Hotel before we'd left Southill. He was the only one with a credit card under a pseudonym, and we hadn't wanted to announce our arrival to anyone who might be tracking our electronic trails. Check-in was at four in the afternoon, so he'd called the night concierge, a gentleman named Robert, with the confirmation number and asked for an early check-in. Thankfully, because of the vacancies, he'd given us the green light without charging us for an extra night.

I gripped the wheel tightly as we closed in on the downtown area and spouted some non-relevant facts to calm my nerves. "Did you know that Eureka Springs has one of the largest collections of Victorian homes and buildings in the central U. S., and almost every place downtown is listed in the National Register of Historic Places?"

"Guess we better not blow anything up then," Carver said.

"Probably a good idea," I agreed, ignoring the slight accusation in his voice. We were both upset and reacting to his dig would've started a fight that neither of us had time for.

"Sorry," he muttered.

"Apology accepted," I said sincerely.

I exited left onto Spring Street. The 1905 Basin Park Hotel was on the left just before the famous wedge-looking Flatiron building that stood between Spring and Center Streets. It was nestled into a hill-side by the Basin Park Spring, with a rough lime-stone and dolomite exterior. I'd read on the website that the original hotel, The Perry House, had burned down in 1890, and this structure had been built in its place to be fireproof.

Ironic since I was wielding some unpredictable fire magic. I hoped the place was fireproof enough to survive me for a few days.

I parked across the street in the yellow loading zone and turned off the engine. According to the website, we had ten minutes to check in, get our parking pass, get our bags to our rooms, and move the car to the hotel parking lot several streets away. It was a lot, but we'd chosen the place for its central location.

Carver gathered a small carry-on and his spell-crafting bag before exiting the car and heading across the street to the hotel lobby entrance. I glanced at Zev and held my hand out. He laced his fingers in mine.

"We should get inside," I said.

"My contact just texted." He nodded at the hotel.

"Doesn't Carver have the recording?" I asked.

"I recorded a copy on my phone," he replied. "You go on while I text back with the information about the recording."

"But I want to know what he says." I was eager to know if the foreign language was the key to turning the tide on our situation, but also, Zev had been almost secretive about his 'contact,' careful not to use any pronouns, and I wanted to see if he would correct me.

He didn't.

"It will take some time to get the translation back," he assured me. "Go on. I'll get the bags and bring them in when I'm done here."

I had an uneasy feeling I couldn't shake. "Don't take too long."

"I won't," he promised.

The uneasiness didn't disappear as I grabbed my purse and crossed to the hotel lobby. I'd tied Rowan's tennis shoes tightly, but the extra toe room was distracting. I glanced back at my car, and Zev was still in the passenger seat.

"Elena," Carver called out while waving at me. Elena was the name I'd decided on in the car. Carver's pseudonym was Stefan Almadori, and I'd recently binged *The Vampire Diaries* a few weeks earlier when I'd been missing Zev. The name had popped out of my mouth before I could stop myself. "I've got our room keys and a parking pass."

He stood in front of a vintage concierge desk. A Black man in a light gray button-down shirt, which could have been pink for all I knew, stood behind the desk, his face beaming with pleasure as he gave me a welcoming smile.

His name badge said Robert, confirming he was the person Carver had talked to on the phone. "Hi, Robert," I greeted him. "Thanks for letting us in early."

"My pleasure, Elena," he replied. To his credit, he didn't even blink at my oversized peasant blouse dress or the too-big tennis shoes I wore with it. He was generously warm in demeanor. "As I told Stefan, once you folks get the car to the hotel parking lot, just call for a shuttle. One will come right over and pick you up." He handed me three cards. "Here are your Daily Resort Passes. They give you access to the spa sun deck and hot tub, three tickets to the Peculiar Things & Remarkable Springs Tour, and shuttle service throughout the downtown area. Wifi is included in the price."

"Thanks, Robert." We weren't here for vacation, but the shuttle service passes could be useful in getting around town inconspicuously. Just some tourists doing touristy stuff. "We'll get our bags upstairs and get out of your hair."

"If you folks are hungry, we serve breakfast in our restaurant between eight and eleven, and room service is twenty-four hours a day."

My stomach growled at the mention of food. "Thanks. We'll definitely check it out."

Carver glanced at the front door. "What's keeping Damon?"

"He was, uh, responding to a text."

Carver's expression lit up.

I nodded. "Yep, *that* text." Though surely, he was finished by now. "I'll go check on him." I excused myself, then strode to the door. Looking out the window, I let out a string of curses that would've made a sailor blush.

Carver rushed over. "What's wrong?"

"I'm going to kill him," I seethed. "Then when he comes back to life, I'm going to kill him again."

Carver looked confused momentarily as he stared out the window on the door. "Where's the car?"

"Exactly." I swore if Zev was doing something stupid, like trying to figure out a way to get himself trapped to save my brother, I was going to light his djinn ass on fire.

Chapter Six

"I HAVE NO CLOTHES OR ANYTHING," I SAID AS Carver tried, unsuccessfully, to calm me down. Not that anything I'd brought would fit until after the transformational spell ended, but still. "If he was going to take my car and leave, why did he tell me he'd bring my bag in?"

I sucked in a breath. I'd brought my keys in with me, so he'd had to hot-wire my car. If he broke my steering column, or whatever people who hot-wire cars did to steal cars, I was going to break his nose. I dug around in my purse to verify my keys were there. They were not.

I let out a low groan. "I forgot my keys in the car. Why am I so stupid?" I'd basically given him the means and opportunity to enact whatever harebrained scheme he'd concocted. Another terrible thing occurred to me. "My phone! My phone is still connected to the car charger." If Rowan's kidnappers called and I didn't answer... I didn't even want to think about the ramifications for my brother. "I need my phone for the, uhm, call tomorrow."

Carver put his hand on my back. "I'm sure there's a reasonable explanation for—"

I cut him off. "Are you sure? I mean, really sure?" I tried to keep my voice low, but talking softly when enunciating every word to avoid a misunderstanding was hard. "Please tell me the reasonable explanation?" If Zev had disappeared without my car, I might have immediately worried that he'd been snatched, but my car was also missing. And if Zev had been snatched, car and all, wouldn't there have been some kind of commotion? While the ifrit wasn't up to his full power, he could still kick some serious ass. If he'd been taken, why wasn't half the block scorched? "My car is gone, Zev is gone, my phone is gone. There's nothing reasonable about any of that."

"Let's go up to our rooms," Carver said. "Where we can talk privately."

I glared at him but nodded. "Fine. Let's go talk privately."

Concierge Robert cleared his throat. "Excuse me, folks, but is everything okay?"

"Fine," I said, turning on my bright and cheerful

mask. "Everything is great." I looped my arm in Carver's. "Come on, Stefan. Let's go check out our rooms."

We took the elevator to the sixth floor. Carver's suite was old-fashioned but quaint. A four-poster queen-sized bed with a plush goose-down comforter was against the wall, and there was a sitting area with a loveseat and a wingback chair. The carpet was dark with a checkered pattern created with even smaller, darker blocks. Everything was still grayscale, but I imagined the room was decorated in dark greens, burgundies, and blues. Classic Victorian colors. The same colors Rowan had used when he'd restored his home. I crossed the spacious suite to the window and looked out. We were on the fifth floor, and our room had a view of the Flatiron building and most of the historical downtown area.

I pivoted my gaze to the yellow zone, and my stomach knotted. My car and Zev were still gone. "So, what's the reasonable explanation?" I asked Carver.

"Are you kidding me?" was his strained reply. I could hear the rage simmering in his tone. "Zev's obviously made the decision for all of us to go and try to fix this on his own. I swear to the goddess, if Rowan—"

"Hey, hey," I said soothingly. His not-so-calm

demeanor had snapped me out of my shit spiral. "We can't think like that. Whatever Zev is doing, I promise you, he won't let anything happen to Ro. He has already offered to exchange himself for my brother, and that's what the kidnappers want, right? So don't go there, okay." I kept my tone easy-breezy despite the words churning up my fears. "Zev's actions might be misguided, but he wouldn't put Rowan in more danger. You know that."

"I do." Carver took a deep breath. "So, what do we do next?"

"I say we stick with the plan. We have unlimited shuttling, so we go out and see what we can see." I looked down at the charmed ring on his finger. "How's the rabbit?"

"The rabbit?"

"Zzzzzz." I made a buzzing sound and wiggled my index finger in the air.

Carver grinned. "You're bad."

I laughed. "You better believe it."

"It's still vibrating."

"Is it worse when we're close to each other? I mean, does more magic make it vibrate more?"

He arched a brow. "I'm sorry, Mare, but my heart belongs to someone else." My eyes widened at the implication, and Carver chuckled. "Yes," he said. "It does seem to get stronger the closer our proximity."

"Good. That's something, right? You might be able to detect extra magic."

"It's something," he agreed.

I gave his shoulder a light punch. "Thanks, by the way."

"For what?"

"For not letting me panic alone." I hated being treated like Don Quixote, tilting at imaginary windmills. Knowing that Carver shared my fears instantly changed me from a "sky is falling" person into a "we'll figure this out" person. "It's around seven. Too early for the shuttle, and none of the local places will be open. But we should go for a stroll and see if we get any vibes." Walking around town was better than sitting and stewing. "We've only got these bodies for a limited time, so we should make the most of it."

"I'm game. The downtown area isn't that big. It's a good place to start."

"Awesome," I said with less enthusiasm than I was feeling. Now that I'd calmed down, I was worried about Zev. If he had told me what he was doing or where he was going, I would've been angry, but at least I wouldn't be thinking the worst. The not knowing was the worst. "Where the hell is Zev?" I muttered.

"We should try calling him," Carver suggested.

"Oh, yeah, right. Do you have his number?"

"No, I thought you might?"

I shook my head. "Who memorized numbers anymore? However..." I snapped my fingers. "He has my phone." Maybe it wasn't such a bad thing that I'd left it on the charger. "Call it."

Carver took his phone from his pocket and touched the screen. He put the call on speaker. It rang twice, then an automated response said, "The number you have called is unavailable. Please try your call later."

"What the shit?" I balled my hands into fists. "Did he turn my freaking phone off? The nerve!" I danced around on my toes. "I'm going to the bathroom, and then we'll go look around."

I quickly peed, washed my hands, and then splashed some water on my young, unfamiliar face. "Hi, Nikky," I greeted my reflection. The body I was in didn't creak at the knees like the old one, and I had a tenth of the aches and pains. "Thanks for the loan." I didn't linger long. Giving myself a chance to ruminate on how bad our situation had become was counterproductive. With the back of my hand, I wiped at the corner of my eyes. "Big girl panties," I reminded myself, returning to the suite.

"You ready?" Carver asked.

"Born that way," I joked.

The moment we stepped outside, the crisp

morning air hit. I inhaled deeply. "Wow, I can't believe how nice and clean everything smells here. Even your room. You kind of expect an old hotel like this to smell a bit musty."

Carver's stare was incredulous. "You're kidding, right?"

"No." I shook my head and inhaled again. "Everything is so fresh."

"Because our olfactory neurons aren't firing," he said.

I don't know why it struck me as funny, but I choked on a laugh. "That's right. Nose has been turned off." I breathed in again, tasting—or rather not tasting—the air. "Honestly, this is a side effect I could learn to live with."

He splayed his wide palms. "Until you want to enjoy food or fresh herbs or aromatherapy..."

I hadn't thought of that. "True. But until then, I'm going to enjoy this."

The cobblestone streets gleamed and sparkled in the early light, muted in grayscale thanks to the spell's side effects. Eureka Springs was busier than I expected this early in the morning, but just because the local shops didn't open until eight didn't mean there weren't perks to a morning stroll. The charm of the town was wrapped in the stillness of dawn.

Carver's longer legs made it hard for my shorter

ones to keep up. I had to walk double-time, and size five feet in size nine shoes didn't make it any easier.

Carver glanced down at my awkward shuffle, one brow raised. "Still struggling with the sneakers?"

"Oh, you mean the clown boats on my feet?" I gestured dramatically. "Yeah, it's either trip every other step or take them off and risk tetanus. Tough call."

He smirked. "I could carry you."

"You have a baby backpack handy?"

"Yeah, sorry again. I should have picked a different person for you." He scratched his nose. "Maybe I could conjure a carriage or something."

"If we run into a local farmer's market, we'll see if they have any suitable pumpkins." I stumbled again, barely catching myself on a wrought iron lamppost. "If I break this neck, will it still be broken when the spell reverts?"

"Yes," he said. Then, less confidently, added, "You know, I'm not sure."

"Check." I carefully picked up my feet with each step. "Better not take any chances."

Carver chuckled again. "You're always a fun date, Mare."

"Speaking of date..." I cast a sideways glance in his direction. "What's going on with you and my brother?"

His shoulders went back as if I'd threaded a rod through his spine. "Whatever do you mean?"

"The fancy box that only yours or his hand opens."

"A thank-you gift," he said softly. "For letting me stay with him."

"Your bed was made up, and his was messy." When Carver didn't say anything, I added, "I know my brother. Rowan makes his bed first thing. If he'd been sleeping in his bed last, that thing would've had hospital corners, which tells me that someone else was sleeping in his bed, and it sure wasn't Goldilocks."

Carver sighed.

I waved my hand. "You don't have to talk about it. It's your business, yours and Rowan's, but know that if you two are together, I would be your biggest cheerleader. Team Rarver. No, wait, that's terrible. Team Carwan. Better, but still not quite right."

"Stop shipping us," Carver said, but he didn't sound mad. "Rowan isn't ready for anyone to know."

I snapped my fingers. "Duuuude. I knew it! Honestly, you guys are terrible at hiding your insane attraction." I pressed the tip of my two index fingers together and made a zapping sound. "It's electric."

"Rowan's worried, after what happened with

Evan, that Iris and the rest of the family will be disappointed in him."

I gave my friend's back a playful slap. "The way we feel about Evan isn't because the man turned out to be bisexual. It's the fact that he's a cheater-cheater, and he broke my sister's heart. I hope Rowan knows that no matter who he likes or loves, it doesn't change our feelings one little bit. We just want him to be happy. Who cares about the rest?"

"Rowan does." Carver sighed again. "It's okay. Things are... were good between us."

A tear caught in my throat. "We're getting him back. Don't even doubt it."

Carver gave a curt nod. "No doubts."

"Okay, well, pay attention to the magic ring, and let me know if you feel an extra tingle."

"Nothing so far."

We passed a row of tightly packed buildings, with awnings washed in shades of gray. Signs for "The Curious Museum," "Antique Corner," and "The Velvet Fox Tea Room" hung above their respective doors. Their windows displayed dusty trinkets, vintage hats, and old books that looked like they'd fall apart if you so much as breathed on them.

"Of course there's a museum for 'curious' things here. It's like this town was built for Scooby-Doo mysteries." I snorted softly. In an old man's voice, I said, "And we'd have gotten away with it if it wasn't for you meddling kids."

Carver glanced at the tea room. "And for day-drinking grandmas. We should come back for scones if this doesn't end with us all dying horribly."

"Day-drinking Grammy goals for the win," I said, nearly tripping on an uneven cobblestone.

A couple passed us on the sidewalk, each holding a steaming to-go cup of coffee. The woman wore a light jacket, while the man had a camera slung over his shoulder. Tourists, obviously.

I perked up. "Excuse me!"

They paused, both of them blinking at me with mild confusion.

"Hi," I said, plastering on my friendliest smile. "Where'd you get the coffee?"

"Grotto Brew," the woman said, pointing down the street. "Just a block that way."

"Thank you!" I turned to Carver. "We have had very little sleep and need some go-juice, so, come on, caffeine awaits."

"You sure this isn't just an excuse to avoid walking for five more minutes in those shoes?" he asked as we headed in the direction she'd pointed.

I shrugged. "I'm not too proud to admit it."

Grotto Brew turned out to be a tiny coffee shop tucked into the side of a weathered brick building.

There were two bistro tables with chairs on the sidewalk. Its wooden sign swung gently in the breeze, and when we walked inside, I expected the scent of roasted coffee beans to hit me like a warm hug. It did not, thanks to my broken smeller.

"Bummer."

"Told you," Carver said, giving me a gentle nudge. "Being able to smell comes in handy sometimes."

"When you're right, you're right." Inside, exposed brick, mismatched furniture, and string lights lent the space a cozy, bohemian feel—just my speed.

I stepped up to the counter, suddenly self-conscious as I caught the barista's curious gaze. She was a petite woman with sharp features that included a nose ring, dark wavy hair pinned back, and a crescent moon tattoo with an elaborate flourish design under it on her left wrist. She greeted us with a smile that felt warm, but her sharp eyes lingered a second too long.

Carver tapped his finger on the counter, and I looked down. It was the enchanted ring finger.

"Getting buzzed," I murmured under my breath.

He gave me a sidelong glance. "Yep."

"What'll it be?" the barista asked, her voice warm and curious.

"Double espresso," Carver said.

"Same," I added. "Plus, whatever pastry will make me feel like I have my life together."

The barista's laugh was light but edged with something harder to place. She wrapped up a cinnamon swirl scone. "This one won't fix your life, but it'll sure take the edge off." She slid it across the counter. "Be right back with those espressos."

When she stepped away to work the espresso machine, I leaned toward Carver. "It's buzzing more, isn't it?"

"Yes," he said softly. "But let's not jump to conclusions. She probably doesn't have anything to do with Rowan."

"Or," I countered, barely moving my lips, "she could be the kidnapper's magical coffee-slinging accomplice."

"Occam's razor, Mare," Carver whispered.

"And what's that, exactly?"

"The simplest explanation is usually the right one. It's more likely she's a kitchen witch or something akin to one, trying to live her best barista life."

I glanced at the barista again. She caught my eye and gave me a polite smile. "Almost done," she said, taking the cups from the machine and walking them back to the counter. "That'll be eighteen dollars."

"More like a highway robbery witch," I muttered

as she took the twenty-dollar bill Carver gave her and walked to the cash register to make change.

"Keep the change," Carver said to her, taking his coffee from the counter. "Drink your scone and eat your coffee. Or whichever way you want to do it."

I rolled my eyes but took my cup and pastry. Outside, we sat at one of the bistro tables.

"Are you still buzzing hard?"

"Nope," he admitted. "She was definitely magical."

I couldn't shake the feeling we'd just met someone who could help us find Rowan, though whether she was a friend or foe remained to be seen.

"We're coming back to question her," I said firmly.

Carver shrugged. "You're the boss."

"I'm glad we've established hierarchy." I met his gaze. "Seriously, though. She might know something or have seen something. By the way, why did you think she was a kitchen witch?"

"Her tattoo." He shrugged. "I know a coven of kitchen witches in Illinois, and that's the sign of their coven. It could be a coincidence, but with her being magical and having that specific ink, I don't think it is."

"Well, better for us if she is." I sipped the espresso, disappointed that the lack of scent made it bitter. I gestured toward the door. "If I was the only witch in this town, I think I would notice if supernatural strangers had invaded."

The barista walked out as I said that last part and mused, "I have noticed. And those strangers are you. What business do you have in my neck of the woods?" She held up a finger. "Make it good, sweethearts, because otherwise, I'll have you on the first bus out of town, and don't think I can't make good on my word."

Well, crap. The shit show was ramping up for its second act.

Chapter Seven

"I'm Veronica Dale," the barista said, grabbing a chair from a nearby table and setting it between Carver and me. She sat down like she had all the time in the world, crossing her arms and pinning us with a sharp, expectant look.

I leaned back in my seat, matching her energy. "You first."

She smirked, but her eyes stayed wary. "I don't think the two of you are in any position to negotiate."

"Oh, I don't know about that," I said loudly enough to turn a few heads. More quietly, I added, "Unless you want everyone in town to know you're a witch." I stretched the word like it was the juiciest gossip I'd ever shared. "Do they still hunt them around here?"

Veronica's smirk faltered for a fraction of a

second. She nonchalantly glanced at two men crossing the street nearby. She didn't fool me. She might not have seemed rattled, but I could tell she didn't want the entire town knowing her business. "Cute. Fine." She leaned forward slightly. "I'll go first. I'm a witch. Now it's your turn to tell me what you are."

Carver leaned in close. "How did you know we're not normal?"

That was an excellent question. We were under a spell that was supposed to protect us from prying eyes. Transformations that were supposed make it difficult to identify us. "Yeah," I said. "What gave us away?"

Veronica tilted her head, her gaze flicking to Carver's hand. "The ring. I could feel its magical vibration the second you walked in. Damn thing's loud enough to wake the dead."

I snorted. "That's what she said."

Carver groaned but cracked a smile as he shook his head.

"What?" I asked innocently.

He looked cross as he slipped the ring off and put it on the table. "It hadn't even crossed my mind that the talisman was a freaking neon sign. I could've blown this for us. Maybe I already have."

"We're okay." I put my hand on his. "Looks like

we're going to have to chuck the ring into the nearest trash can, though."

"You two lovebirds hash it out later," Veronica said. "Because now it's your turn. How'd you peg me as a witch?"

"The ring," Carver told her, then he nodded at her wrist. "And your tattoo. It's the same design the Sisters of the Bloom in Illinois use. I helped their coven last year with a blight curse on their greenhouses."

Veronica's eyes widened. "No shit? I grew up with the Sisters of the Bloom. My mom's the coven leader."

"Delphia is your mother? Small world," Carver said, his tone warming. "I'm an eclectic witch. I take on jobs for all sorts, removing curses and hexes, protection spells, stuff like that. It's my specialty."

"And he's the best at it," I said. "He's renowned in magical circles."

Her mouth twitched like she didn't quite believe him, and she pulled out her phone. "Let's see."

She hit speed dial and put the call on speaker. A cheerful voice answered. "Vee? It's awful early, sweetheart. Is everything okay?"

"Hey, Mom. I've got someone here who says he worked with the Sisters of the Bloom last year."

"Carver Martin," Carver said quietly.

"Did you hear that, Mom? Carver Martin. Does that name ring a bell?"

There was a brief pause. "Yes," she answered. "He helped us with an awful blight curse that a mischievous fairy put on our greenhouses. He's a gifted eclectic witch. Why? Are you hiring him?" Delphia suddenly sounded worried. "Has someone hexed you?"

"Mooom," Veronica whined. "It's not like that. I'm fine. No hexes." She arched an eyebrow at Carver, who gave her a small, satisfied smile. "Can you tell me what he looks like? For verification."

"Uh, sure, honey," her mom said. "He's tall, lanky, with messy dark hair and a hawkish nose. No offense, Carver."

"My nose is my nose, Delphia," he replied. "No offense taken."

Veronica slowly lowered the phone and stared at him. "That's not what he looks like." She snapped a picture.

I jumped in before she could send it by thrusting my hand out for her to shake. "I'm Carver's new partner." That wasn't entirely a lie. Veronica ignored my offered hand, but she didn't do anything with the photo either, so I was calling it a win. "I'm also an eclectic witch, and we're undercover in town. There are some... uh, bad people who took... something.

Something that doesn't belong to them." I glanced at Carver. "And the original owners want it back. These people are powerful, so we used a spell to change our appearances to keep our presence in the area undetected. As I'm sure your mom can attest, Carver is very well known, and his real appearance makes him hard to miss."

Veronica didn't look fully convinced. "How do I know you're telling the truth?"

"Ask your mom," Carver said calmly.

Veronica raised the phone again. "Mom, how can I verify he's the same Carver Martin who helped you?"

"Ask how he was paid," her mom said without missing a beat.

Veronica's gaze shifted back to us. "Well?"

I assumed the answer was money, but I couldn't have been more wrong.

"I was paid two ounces of blessed sargol—red stigma saffron grown on sacred goddess ground," Carver answered smoothly.

Her jaw dropped. "Wait. Are you serious? That's how you were paid? Do you know how expensive that is?" She held up three fingers. "Each flower produces only three stigmas. Two ounces is... well, that's ridiculous."

"He's Carver Martin," Delphia said. "That deal

was between him and me alone. Not even the other coven members know."

Veronica reassessed Carver, eyeballing him up and down, then nodded. "Impressive." To Delphia, she said, "Thanks, Mom. Call you soon." She ended the call, looking impressed for the first time. "Okay, I believe you."

"And?" I prompted, leaning forward.

"And I'll help you," Veronica said. "Who or what are you looking for?"

I hesitated. Her willingness to help was a step forward, but my stomach twisted when I thought of Zev. Where was he? What was he doing? He'd already made it clear he'd sacrifice himself if it meant saving Rowan. That was what scared me the most.

I tried not to dwell on it. Worrying wouldn't help find him or Rowan, but shutting it off was hard. I pressed my fingers against my temple and tried to reach out with my thoughts, the way Zev had done with me in Natheria. *Zev, if you can hear me, I'm worried about you. Just... send me something.*

Nothing came back. No flicker of emotion, no reassuring voice. Just the endless swirl of my own crap.

Carver nudged me gently with his elbow, snapping me back to reality. "Mare? You good?"

"Yeah," I said quickly, brushing it off. "Let's focus on finding Rowan."

Veronica's sharp gaze flicked between us. "So, you're looking for a who, not a what?"

"What will your services cost?" Carver asked.

Veronica grinned as she scooted forward in her chair. "Nothing much." She poked the ring with her index finger, then lifted her hand, and it slid down her slender finger. "I'll take this little trinket in exchange."

I looked at Carver, and he gave me an almost imperceptible nod. Before I agreed to the kitchen witch's terms, though, I had a term of my own. I guessed she was about five foot six, but she was slender, and her feet were small. "Agreed," I told her. "On one condition."

She raised her brows. "And that would be?"

"I want your clothes and your shoes."

Veronica scoffed. "You want me to strip right here?"

"If that's how you want to play it." I sighed. "Look. I'm normally six feet two inches, and I'm definitely not a size zero with size five feet, and unfortunately, there's not an all-night Walmart between here and Southill, and I'm in serious need of clothes that won't make me stick out like a sore thumb or shoes that will get me killed because I can't walk in them."

She laughed. "I just thought you had a terrible sense of style."

"Not usually," I told her. "Come on. Help a sister out."

"Six foot two, huh?" Finally, she shrugged. "Okay, sure. Why not? I keep the ring, you get new clothes, we find the who, and bah-dah boom, presto-chango, all is right with the world."

I only wished it was that easy. "We can start with the ring and clothes."

"Come on," she said. "My apartment is upstairs. I'll tell Nelly I'm taking the day off. It's slow on weekdays, anyhow."

"You own the coffee shop?" I asked as we followed her back inside.

"Yep," she answered. "Lock, stock, and two steaming mocha lattes."

Ten minutes later, I stood in Veronica's apartment, staring at myself in a full-length mirror.

The space was dramatic, and my inability to see color made it seem even more so. The walls were a deep gray, almost black, but the trim and ceiling beams were stark white, giving the space a crisp edge. A black velvet chaise lounge sat near a window framed with gauzy, sheer curtains, and the small coffee table in front of it was topped with an assortment of candles—black, white, and gray—along with a stack of books about herbs, magic, and Victorian occult practices. The bookshelf against one wall was filled with neat rows of books, a few framed photos, and an assortment of sleek black cat figurines.

Her kitchen was small but immaculate, with black countertops and shiny silver appliances gleaming even in the low light. A few various shades of gray plants, mostly succulents, were clustered on the windowsill, adding their own touch to the moody decor.

"This is not my idea of blending in," I said, looking at my new duds in the mirror. I had on black leggings, a black and white tunic dress over them, and black combat boots. "I look like Goth Barbie."

"Barbie would have bigger boobs," Veronica replied. "Besides, I think you look more like the Keebler Elf."

I frowned. "Elf?"

"With all that green, you only need pointy shoes and a hat, and the outfit would be complete."

Okay, so not black tights and a black and white tunic. I wasn't sure Keebler Elf was much better, though.

Carver put his hand over his mouth to cover a snicker.

"It's not funny," I told him.

He grinned. "It's not-not funny."

"You're terrible."

"I have my moments." He laughed.

It made me laugh.

"You two are adorable," Veronica said. "How long have you been together?"

That made us laugh even harder.

When I could breathe again, I told her, "We're not together. We're just friends."

"Sure," she said.

"I'm gay," Carver said flat out.

"That's cool. Love is love." Veronica shrugged. "Besides, I've been known to dabble."

"And," Carver continued, "I'm in love with her brother."

That had my eyebrows going up. "In love, huh?"

"Yes," he said, his tone turning more serious. "He's the missing person we're trying to find."

"I have a boyfriend as well," I told her, even though having a 'boyfriend' sounded weird at my age, but saying he was my lover would've been even weirder. "He's missing too."

"You all are having trouble keeping track of your men. Maybe I should charge you two rings."

Carver's gaze narrowed on her. "The ring is platinum. Even without it being charmed, it's worth a lot of money. With the charm, it's a small fortune. You can take that as payment, or we can call our bargain done. I don't renegotiate a contract once the terms have been set."

"I was just joking. No harm, no foul." She held up her hands in submission. A real black cat strolled out from Veronica's bedroom. "It's nice of you to join us, Mr. Whispers." Her smile widened. "He must've decided you guys were all right."

"Mr. Whispers?"

"It's ironic," she said. "He yowls all night long. I've threatened to gag him more than once."

I chuckled. "Hello, Mr. Whispers," I told him. "It's nice to meet you."

He meowed a greeting back and rubbed his face against my offered hand.

I tucked my chin. "Could you say that again?"

Mr. Whispers *myipped* as a response.

I couldn't understand anything he was saying, which meant the transformation had blocked my ability to talk to animals—a talent I'd developed since becoming part forest giant.

"If you're waiting for him to talk like Salem from Sabrina the Teenage Witch, you're going to be waiting a long time. She laughed. "Mr. Whispers is a nosy cat, but he doesn't speak human." She crossed her legs in her seat and the cat jumped into her lap. Stroking his fur, she asked, "Tell me how you tracked your missing persons to Eureka Springs?"

"It wasn't hard. We got a text from the kidnappers saying to meet them here in two days, that was a day ago. They want to do a prisoner exchange. Basically, my man for my brother."

Veronica grunted, catching the gist. "And your man is missing?"

"Yes." I sat on a stool near the floor-length mirror. "He disappeared when we first arrived in town."

"Do you think he ran?" she asked.

"No." I shook my head. "I think he's trying to find a way to trade himself for Rowan before anyone gets hurt."

"Noble," Veronica commented.

"And stupid," I amended.

"Of course." She nodded. "Very stupid."

"Men," I harrumphed.

"The worst," she agreed.

"Man in the room," Carver jumped in.

Veronica giggled. "Solidarity, sister," she said out of the side of her mouth.

It made me smile. "How about we tell you what we know, and you can tell us if you can help."

"You know I'm keeping the ring either way, right?" She stroked the ring and mimicked Gollum. "My preciousssss."

Carver leaned forward, his eyes intense. "You know it's never a good idea to accept something for nothing from an eclectic witch, right? You'll pay either in help or..." he kept his gaze steady. "I'll exact payment in other ways."

Veronica was frozen like a deer in the headlights for a moment. Then she shook her arms and said, "Of course, I'm going to help. Tell me what you got."

I explained in detail everything relevant that had happened since I'd seen the text, from calling Carver, the transformation potion, and the recording in Rowan's office.

"Wait," Veronica said, her eyes lit up with excitement. "He described a guy with long white hair that was pulled up into a top knot."

"Yeah," I said eagerly. "Driving a white SUV. Do you know who it is?"

"Not who, but I've seen him around. He's kind of hard to miss. He looks like a fitness model. The kind you'd see on a romance novel. Hot, hot, and, wow, sizzling hot."

"Where did you see him?" Carver asked. "Did you talk to him? Do you know where he's staying?"

"It's not like he took me to his home and banged my brains out," she said but gave us a cagey smile. "Not to say that I didn't try to flirt with him. But the man engaged less than a guard at Buckingham Palace. He wouldn't even make eye contact with me."

"But...." I rolled my hand at her.

"But..." she grinned. "I might have seen the SUV heading toward The Grand Treehouse Resort on West Van Buren." She spread her hands. "I can't guarantee that he's there, but the resort is basically a bunch of treehouse cabins. And they are far enough apart that there's some privacy. It could be the perfect place to hide a kidnapping victim."

"My brother's not a victim."

"Sorry," Veronica said. "Poor choice of words."

"No, I'm sorry for snapping." The kitchen witch had given us our first tangible clue to Rowan's where-abouts, and she deserved better from me. "This is a lead. A real one. I'm so grateful, I can't even tell you."

"So..." Veronica rubbed her hands together. "Are we going or what?"

"What?" Carver asked.

"Well, you don't have a car. The trolley doesn't run out that way, and I am better than Uber." She smiled. "So, what do you say?"

"I say, hell yes," I told her.

Carver stood up. "We'll follow you."

"Awesome." Veronica gave a little fist pump.

I wasn't sure if I was charmed by her excitement or disturbed, but for the first time, it felt like we were moving in the right direction—and that was enough for now.

Chapter Eight

Veronica's car was a hybrid electric sedan. "Doing my part for the environment," she said as we walked three blocks to the parking lot where she kept it.

When I'd complained about the distance, she told us, "There aren't a lot of places for parking in downtown Eureka Springs," she continued. "Even locals have to pay to park, just like the tourists. Ugh."

"I would hate having to walk a quarter mile to get to my car every day," I told her, feeling a pang of sympathy.

"I work in the same building where I live," she chuckled. "In other words, I don't drive much. Most of the time, I just take the trolley wherever I need to go. Honestly, it would be cheaper for me to rent a car when I needed to leave town than to keep one, but I bought this baby when I moved away from Illinois, and I just can't bring myself to let it go."

The Grand Treehouse Resort was on the northwestern edge of town. Veronica drove us down South Main Street and turned right onto West Van Buren Road—Highway 62 West. It was the same road we'd taken into Eureka Springs.

As we neared our destination, a familiar billboard caught my eye. "Hey, I saw that sign on the way in." Remembering it made my chest squeeze. "We might've driven right by the place where my brother was being held prisoner."

Carver, sitting in the back seat, gave us the play-by-play. "When we get there, we go in, drive around, and if anyone asks, we're tourists loving Eureka Springs and simply checking out other places to stay for our next visit."

I gave him a thumbs up. "I've memorized the script."

He flicked the back of my head lightly. "Smart ass."

"Ow," I whimpered, rubbing the spot even though it didn't hurt.

"Whimp," Carver teased. "I barely tapped you."

Veronica glanced at me, then back at Carver through the rearview mirror. "Okay, now I see it. At first, I thought you two were giving couple vibes, but this is definitely bestie chemistry."

I snorted but didn't deny it. She wasn't wrong.

When we pulled into The Grand Treehouse Resort, I realized it was even more secluded than I'd imagined. Especially considering how close it was to town. The place was small, with only six treehouse-style cabins generously spaced out in the dense four-and-a-half acre woodland. Tall trees surrounded each cabin, their leaves forming a canopy that isolated them from the populated areas of Eureka Springs. The cabins each had their own unique designs, but thanks to the potion messing with our senses, I couldn't tell if the buildings were techni-color or not. It was a grayscale paradise of trees. Lots and lots of trees.

Veronica drove slowly along the asphalt drive, her hands gripping the steering wheel tightly as she squinted at the cabins tucked among the dense trees. Each one had its own unique design, from wrap-around decks to quirky little staircases leading to their doors, but one detail was the same...every single cabin had a white SUV parked out front.

I leaned forward, pressing my hands against the dashboard. "Man, white SUVs are either super popular, or whoever has Rowan booked the entire place." My gaze darted from one cabin to the next.

"Does that mean there are six bad guys, each wanting their own beds, or a small army of them buddying up in these cozy little hideouts?"

Carver shifted in the back seat, leaning closer to get a better look out the window. His lips pressed into a thin line. "I wouldn't be surprised if they booked the entire resort. They'd want privacy, especially if they're planning to trap a djinn. But they'd also want to stay close enough to town for tomorrow when you were supposed to arrive."

Veronica, eyes wide, slammed her foot, bringing the car to a jarring halt. "Wait a minute," she said sharply. "Rowan is a djinn? Djinns are real?"

Her reaction caught me off guard. I waved my hand quickly, hoping to calm her down. "No, not Rowan. He's a doctor. And an eclectic witch in training. But yes, djinns are real."

Veronica's expression didn't soften as her gaze flicked between me and Carver. "Then who's the djinn?" she asked suspiciously.

I hesitated, my hands fidgeting with the hem of my tunic. The ache in my chest tightened. "That would be my man."

"The one who went missing?" she pressed.

"Yep," I confirmed, forcing myself to look away from the cabins as if that would ease the rising anxiety inside me. "He's the one these jackholes want. He's the reason they decided to take my brother."

Veronica's hands loosened slightly on the wheel as she processed this. "Because this djinn loves you?" she asked cautiously, her voice quieter now.

"Among other things," I replied vaguely, leaning back in my seat. I wasn't about to launch into the messy details of the soul fragment I shared with Zev. Was it even working anymore? Since the transformation spell, I hadn't accidentally set anything on fire. Was that because the magic blocking our sense of smell and ability to see color also blocked my connection to Zev? He'd read my mind in the car, right? But that had been before the side effects of the spell kicked in. Maybe he was trying to reach me, but I just couldn't sense him because of the potion's magic. Sadly, this possibility didn't make me feel better, but at least it was something.

Carver cleared his throat loudly, breaking the silence and pulling me from my spiraling thoughts. "First things first, we need to figure out who these people are."

"This would've been a great time for Zev to come through with a translation," I muttered, slumping against the seat in frustration.

"But he hasn't," Carver said matter-of-factly. He

leaned forward, his hands gripping the back of my seat. "So we're doing this the old-fashioned way."

"And that would be?" I craned my neck to look back at him.

His expression was deadpan. "We're getting out and knocking on doors."

My response was just as deadpan with a hint of genuine concern. "Are you nuts?"

"A little," he admitted with a shrug. "Right now, they don't know who we are. We'll be the most annoying tourists ever and see how far we can push it before they kick us out of the resort."

"Or get rid of us permanently," Veronica interjected as the voice of reason.

I didn't buy it. I smirked at her. "You know you want to knock on doors."

Veronica's lips curled into a mischievous grin, and she held up her hands. "Guilty as charged," she admitted. "Just playing Devil's advocate. I'm totally on board for this suicide mission."

I narrowed my gaze at her. "Why?"

"Why what?" she asked, her grin fading.

"Why are you on board?" I folded my arms and tilted my head, waiting for her answer.

She paused, the corners of her lips twitching upward again. "Because bored is the operative word. This is the most excitement I've had in... well, longer than I can remember. I didn't move away from my coven for quilting bees and knitting circles."

My brow furrowed. "How did you end up in Eureka Springs?"

Her laugh was soft but knowing, and she shifted in her seat. "A man."

I couldn't help laughing. "No explanations necessary." I gestured toward the cabins. "We might as well start at the last one and work our way to the exit."

Veronica eased us further down the driveway to our first destination. "Here we go," she mumbled nervously.

Carver was out of the car before the engine was fully off, stretching his legs and eyeing the cabin like he was gearing up for battle.

I turned to Veronica. "You don't have to knock on doors with us. Actually, it's probably safer if you don't. After all, we're in disguise. You're not. When this is all over, you'll still look like you."

Veronica's chin lifted, and her expression turned defiant. "Forget it. I'm doing this with you and seeing it through to the end. I have to earn my payment."

Her comment about payment reminded me of the ring. "Wait. You better leave the ring in the car. Otherwise, they might detect the magic the same way you did."

Veronica blinked, then nodded. "Good idea." She tugged the ring off her finger and slipped it into the cupholder.

Carver rapped his knuckles on the passenger window, his face set in an exasperated "are you getting out?" expression.

I pushed the door open and climbed out, taking in the quiet surroundings. The cabin's porch loomed above us, and the faint sound of pine branches rustling in the breeze was the only noise breaking the stillness.

Veronica joined us, rubbing her palms against her leggings. "Sweaty hands," she complained. "It's hereditary."

"We'll be sisters," I told her. "Minus the hereditary palm sweats." I flashed her a smile. "My husband and I are visiting you from out of town, and you're taking us around to do the tourist crap."

"Got it," Veronica replied. "I memorized the script too."

I smirked. "You know, that does sound a little smart-assy."

"See," Carver said. "I told you."

We followed Carver up the steep steps to the front door.

"You want me to take the lead?" I asked.

"You're better with people, so have at it." He gave me a quick wink. "Ready?"

"Let's get this party started." Without further ado, I knocked on the door.

It opened to reveal a man so large I almost took a step back. He had to be six foot five, with light hair spiked up with gel, dark eyes that radiated danger, and arms like tree trunks. Two scars cut down either side of his face, and his scowl was the epitome of intimidating.

"What do you want?" he barked.

I immediately plastered on my best southern-belle smile. "We're here in Eureka Springs for the first time visiting my sissy, and I can't tell you how much we've fallen in love with this place. Bless my husband's heart, he wanted to check out all the places to stay, and these treehouse cabins are so charming. We stopped in hoping to get a peek around and see if the inside matches the out."

My smile could've melted diamonds. His expression stayed unmoved.

"No," he said bluntly. "Go away."

Before he could shut the door, I slapped my hand on it. My heart thudded against my ribs, and a semi-joking voice in my head whispered, *You're going to get murdered, Marigold. This guy is going to murder you and everyone you love.* But I didn't back down.

"You seem like a reasonable man," I said sweetly. "Just one quick little turn around. It wouldn't take a sec."

The man growled, low and guttural. "You go or else."

I swallowed hard but kept my smile in place. "Now, no need to be rude and unneighborly."

The man crossed his arms, his muscles bulging under his sleeves. A string of tattoos ran down the outer edges of his forearms, resembling hieroglyphs. One in particular caught my attention—an oval with an upside-down triangle and something that looked like horns.

Carver stepped in, adopting a thick accent. "No, honeybunches, let's leave the nice man to his vacation. Maybe one of the guests in the other cabins will let us take a quick gander."

I tried craning my neck to look around the man, but my short stature made it impossible to see past his brick wall body. "Fine," I huffed. "We'll try someone else."

The man's voice dropped to an icy growl. "Don't come back, or you will wish you never had."

He slammed the door in our faces. Carver quickly ushered me down the steps, one hand on my back as he kept glancing over his shoulder. Veronica was already halfway to the car.

Once we were back inside, Carver turned to me, his voice urgent. "Did you hear it?"

I buckled my seatbelt, my pulse still racing. "I heard that he was an asshole, if that's what you mean."

"No." Carver shook his head, his eyes intense. "The threat at the end. Did you hear it? Marigold, I think he's the man Rowan recorded. I think that's the person who took him."

My heart lurched. "Are you sure?"

"I've listened to the recording over and over, hoping to find something else. When he started to talk, I thought he sounded familiar, but when he said that last bit, I knew for sure."

Hope surged inside me, hot and desperate. Were we actually close to finding Rowan? But reality hit me hard. Even if we were, how in the world could we get him away from that guy without getting ourselves and Rowan killed in the process?

"Uh, guys," Veronica said, her voice tight. "We have trouble."

Carver and I turned in unison. My stomach dropped as another white SUV pulled up behind us, blocking the only way out. Two more men stepped out, both as big and intimidating as the first guy, their eyes locked on us.

"Okay," I whispered, gripping the edge of my seat. "Now what?"

The big man from the cabin came down the steps to the vehicle. "You have two choices," he told us. "Drive yourself away, or my men will throw your bloody, bruised, unconscious bodies out."

Veronica frowned and gave a headshake. "We'll take option A," she told him, starting her car. "I like driving. Driving is good."

He stepped back and gestured at the men blocking our exit. They got back into their SUVs and made a hole. Veronica, without another word, drove out of The Grand Treehouse Resort like the Devil himself was on our ass.

My eyes watered, and I blinked at Carver. "That man is one scary bastard."

"He paints a vivid picture," he agreed. "At least he let us go."

"And I'm never going back there again," Veronica stated. "That dude has serious anger management issues, and I like my face the way it is."

I liked my face as well, but if it meant rescuing Rowan, I was definitely going back. This time, I would avoid the front door.

Carver glanced at me, his voice low. "We're going to need a better plan."

"The kind of plan that breaks all the rules," I

said, my heart hammering in my chest. If we were going to get Rowan back, we'd have to outsmart these guys at their own game.

In this new body, the triangles on my hand where I'd absorbed Zev's soul had disappeared with the transformation, but suddenly, they flared to life, burning the symbols into the pale skin I wore.

I reached back and grabbed Carver's hand. "It's him," I said, showing him the burns. "Zev. He must be close."

When we got back to the hotel, my car was again parked out front. Zev, still in disguise, leaned against the hood, his arms crossed over his chest.

"There he is," I hissed, my emotions surging between elation and rage. He was back. He hadn't gotten himself captured. That meant there was still hope.

"That's a djinn?" Veronica asked, confused.

I took a deep breath to clear my head. "It sure is."

"I guess I expected someone more...blue."

I laughed. "Wrong kind of djinn."

Zev was back, and we had a lot more information than when we'd left Southill Village, including a possible location. We'd rescue Rowan. There was no other choice.

This wasn't over. Not even close.

Chapter Nine

"Sooo," Veronica cooed as she rolled to a stop. "That's a djinn, huh? Where do I rub to get three wishes?"

"Rub him anywhere, and you'll be wishing you still had a hand," I told her, only half-joking.

She laughed. "Got it. Keep my paws to myself."

This time it was me instead of Carver who got out of the car before the engine shut down. I forced myself to walk, not run, to Zev. When I was a few feet away, he pushed away from the car and straightened up.

"Where in the hell did you go?"

He gave me a quizzical look. "I'm not sure what you mean?"

Flabbergasted, I said, "What do you mean you're not sure what I mean?"

"Are you saying you know me?"

"Don't play dumb with me, Zev."

He grimaced. "My name is Zev?"

Goddess help me, I was going to throat-punch the man. "Are you saying you don't remember your name?"

"Look, Miss..."

"It's Marigold," I told him. The fact that he didn't look or sound like Zev had me questioning what I knew to be the truth. Unless Carver's donor showed up in Eureka Springs and happened to coincidentally stand by my car that had been missing for a couple hours, then this was Zev. "Don't mess with me."

"I'm not trying to, and if you say I'm this Zev that you know, then I'm inclined to believe you, but it doesn't change the fact that I don't remember."

Carver had joined us. "What's the last thing you do remember?"

"A few minutes ago, I woke up in the passenger seat of this car." He patted the hood. "Nothing before then."

"Nothing?" I asked. My skin began to itch. I turned sharply to Carver. "Could this be another side effect of the spell?"

He looked constipated as he scratched his jaw. "I don't think so, but...it's possible."

My voice raised an octave. "Are you freaking kidding me?"

"Hold up," Zev said. "Spell?" He peered at us suspiciously. "Are you part of a cult? Did you drug me? Is that why I can't remember anything?"

"Calm down," I said, as if those two words ever calmed anyone down. And honestly, I was talking more to myself than Zev or Carver. "We're not part of a cult, and we certainly didn't drug you. You know us." I tried to take his hand, but he pulled away. My heart broke a little. "You know me."

"Wait," Carver said. "You woke up in the passenger seat?"

Zev nodded. "Yes."

I opened the driver's side door. My phone was still in its cradle and plugged into the charger. I grabbed it and tried to turn it on, but the battery was dead. Zev's phone was wedged between the passenger seat and the console. I retrieved it to see who he'd been texting with before disappearing, but his phone was dead as well. I slid into the seat and turned the key in the ignition. Nothing. The car battery was dead as well. What had happened when Zev went missing?

"It's like my car was hit by an EMP," I said.

"What's that?" Zev asked.

"An electromagnetic pulse," Veronica said. She

flashed him a brilliant smile. "If you get hit with one of those, you're fresh out of luck."

Zev inclined his head. "Could it have erased my memory?"

"Nah," she told him. "Not unless you got a robot brain." She added, when his expression turned quizzical, "All circuits and wiring instead of blood and brain matter."

He shook his head. "I don't think I'm a robot."

"Definitely not," I assured him. I swallowed the knot in my throat when I noticed he wouldn't look at me. He'd pulled away when I'd tried to take his hand earlier. What had happened to him in those two hours? A small part of me was scared to know, but the biggest part was desperate to find out. "I think we should go somewhere private to talk this through and figure out how we can get your memories back."

"Meanwhile, Rowan is being held by really dangerous men who like to hurt people," Carver said as a reminder. "That has to take priority."

His tone irritated me, but he wasn't wrong. Zev might have lost his memory, but the ifrit was in the least amount of danger between him and my brother. "You're right," I told him. "But we're not going to get into that resort unseen without a plan, so going somewhere private to discuss everything is still a solid idea."

"I'm not going anywhere with you people," Zev said. "I don't want any part of whatever craziness you think is happening here."

"Hey, fella." Veronica linked her arm in his, and I nearly came out of my skin when he didn't pull away from her. "No one wants to hurt you. You can see these two know you pretty, well, and while I've just met them, I think they're a bit of all right. So come with us, and I promise, if things get dicey, I'll protect you."

He paused for a moment to consider his options, then finally, met her gaze and nodded. "Okay. However, I might not know much about myself, but I promise, if I'm backed into a corner, I'll come out fighting."

She patted his arm and smirked. "I'd expect nothing less." She ushered him toward the entrance of the hotel.

My scowl deepened. I liked Veronica, but this bitch was about to see my claws if she didn't stop flirting with Zev.

Carver put his hand on my shoulder. "She's helping," he reminded me.

"Helping herself to my man," I muttered. Tamping back my green-eyed monster was hard but doable. Too much was on the line for me to eliminate one of the soldiers in our tiny army... no matter how much I wanted to.

He squeezed. "She's getting him upstairs. I have my spell bag up there, and I might have something that can help him remember who he is."

"Because the last spell you made has worked out so well?" It took everything I had not to roll my eyes or punch the wall.

"We don't know if his amnesia is related. After all, we still have our memories." He stared at me for a long beat. "It's more likely that it happened while he was gone. Wherever he went, whoever he was with, is responsible for his situation. Do you know who his contact was?"

I shook my head. "He was being cagey about it," I admitted. "I don't even know if it was a he, she, zee, or they. He was careful not to even commit to a pronoun."

"Hmmmm." Carver tapped his nose, almost missing the tip because the new nose he wore was smaller than his real one. "And you say the car battery is dead?"

"As a doornail—the car battery and both phones. They might as well be bricks." I winced as reality smacked me hard. "We have to get my phone fixed, or at least get a new one with the same number. If we can't rescue Rowan before the tomorrow morning, I need my phone for when they call."

"Come on," Carver he gestured toward the hotel. "Those two can't go to the rooms without us."

I grabbed mine and Zev's bags from the back seat and threw our phones in for good measure. Carver took Zev's bag, and I slid mine onto my shoulder with my purse before we crossed the street at a quick clip and entered the lobby.

I couldn't shake the unsettling feeling I was missing something. What in the world could erase a djinn's memory? Was it even possible? Of course, it was. After all, Zev had lost his memory. But had he also lost his magic? I flexed my fingers on the hand with the triangles. The brief flash and burn had already healed, and the triangles were gone again. I concentrated on my hand.

"What are you doing?" Carver asked under his breath.

"Trying to make a fireball," I whispered.

"Are you trying to get us kicked out?" he demanded through gritted teeth. He gave Veronica and Zev, waiting by the elevator, a slight wave.

"Nope. I don't think I can even do it right now." I focused on pulling the fire in my veins to let it lose into my palm. The result was a big fat nada. "I haven't accidentally or on purpose started a fire since you put me in this body, and I don't think I can."

"Interesting," Carver said. "The one time I used the transformation spell, I was able to create a potion, but eclectic witches rely on their deities and Mother Earth for magic. Maybe the reason you can't access your fire is because the magic was a part of you, not something you were borrowing from somewhere else."

"That makes sense. You said you changed us down to our DNA. That means that our magical DNA was also transformed." I let out a string of expletives. "I need this stupid spell reversed."

"Can I help you folks?" an older man with gray hair and a mustache asked from behind the front desk.

I dug my key card out of my purse. "Guests." I waved the card in his direction. "We have rooms."

"You can't leave your car in the yellow zone," he said.

"The battery died," I explained. "I'll call for a tow to a mechanic."

That seemed to appease him because he nodded and said, "Have a nice day."

It was way too late for that.

The four of us got on the elevator together. Zev

maintained his distance from me, and I couldn't help but take it personally. I noticed, though, that Veronica was frowning and no longer arm and arm with him. Had he said something to her to back her off? It made me feel the teensiest bit better to think so.

It was a somber and silent ride to the sixth floor. I needed a hot second to myself to process what was going on. It was all too much, and the overwhelm was making it hard to think let alone breathe. "I'll drop the bags off in our room first," I told them. "Then I'll meet you all in Carver's."

I went to my suite as Veronica and Zev followed Carver to his. The room was a different layout, and there was a jetted tub under the window. I threw mine and Zev's bags on the bed then sat on the edge and gave myself thirty seconds to feel my feelings. After that, I'd have to put those emotions into a box and get on with it. Pity parties weren't going to help get Zev's memories or my brother back. I sternly reminded myself this was not about me.

It might not be about me, but I'd been through a hell of a lot recently. The last several days of terror, excitement, mortal danger, rage, and joy rushed through me, and I ugly cried for a solid half minute, give or take a few seconds. It felt cathartic. It wasn't long enough, but time wasn't my friend at the moment. After, I got up, went to the bathroom, and scrubbed my face. Luckily, I wasn't wearing any makeup, not that I ever wore much, but even without the ability to see in color, I could tell by the puffiness around my eyes that they were beet red. I patted my skin dry, then ran cold water over a washcloth and wrung it out. I laid down on the bed and placed the wet cloth over my eyes, the coolness taking the sting out of my heated skin.

A light rap on the door forced me up. "Hold on," I said. I got up, threw the washcloth into the bathroom sink, and opened the door, fully expecting it to be Carver. It wasn't. Instead, Veronica was standing in the hallway, looking slightly embarrassed.

"Hey, Marigold," she greeted. "Can I come in?"

I heaved a sigh but gestured for her to come through. "I was on my way over," I told her.

"Sure," she said. "I just wanted to...you know, say I'm sorry. I wasn't trying to flirt with your fella for bad reasons. I saw the opportunity to help get him to stick around, so I took it."

"Uh huh," I grunted, not buying it. Even so, I wasn't really mad at the young kitchen witch. It was everything else that had my head spinning. "No worries."

"But, uhm, well, I wanted to let you know that when we were in the lobby, he told me he belonged to someone else."

My brow arched. "He did, huh? And who might that be?"

"He said he couldn't remember her name, but he remembered her long black hair, her deep-set brown eyes that spoke to his soul, the curve of her upper lip, one side slightly higher than the other, and that she was tall. Like, over six foot tall." She smiled. "Sound familiar?"

My heart was thumping so hard I could hear it in my ears. "He really said all that?"

"Yes," she told me. "So, even if he doesn't know..." she waved her hand, gesturing to my current appearance, "...this you. Honey, let me tell you, that man knows you." She dipped her head at me. "We okay?"

"Yeah," I told her. "We're good. We better get to Carver's room before Zev tries to bolt again."

"Good idea." Veronica chuckled. As we left my room, she asked, "Why are all the good men gay or taken?"

I laughed. "Because they're actually good men."

My mood had done a three-sixty. Zev couldn't remember himself, but he could remember me, the real me, and he belonged to me. For now, that was enough. We had bigger fish to fry, and these fish were giant sharks who wouldn't hesitate to eat us. We had to make sure that none of us, including my brother, ended up chum.

Chapter Ten

I grabbed the phones from my bag, along with a couple of charging cables, and followed Veronica down the hall to Carver's suite. Carver sat cross-legged on the floor, his boxy frame hunched over a potion book spread open in his lap. "I'm searching for any semblance of a memory spell," he muttered, flipping through the pages with quick, impatient movements.

Zev stood by the window, his slim shoulders tense as he stared out at the downtown skyline. His light eyes had a faraway, haunted look. It hurt to see him like this.

I handed Carver the phones and cables. "Plug these in. Let's see if they'll take a charge." I turned my attention back to Zev, hesitating before stepping closer. The idea that I made him uncomfortable was devastating, but I couldn't stop myself from asking, "Are you doing okay?"

He turned his head slightly and gave me a tired, almost apologetic shake of his head. "I'll admit, I'm feeling a bit off-kilter. I just wish I could remember who I am."

Veronica, perched on the arm of a velvet wing-back chair, leaned forward. "Maybe you could share some of your memories with him, Marigold. It might help."

A sad smile tugged at my lips as I recalled the first time we'd met. The memory was so vivid it felt like yesterday. "The first time I saw you, you came to my sister Iris's house," I began. "She'd just discovered she was a tru-craft witch. She could control the elements, and she'd sparked to fire, but hadn't been able to use it at the time. You were there to test her."

Zev furrowed his brow, his gaze sharpening slightly. "I was doing what?"

"You're an ifrit," I said softly. "A creature of fire."

He gave a dry laugh. "You have to know how ridiculous that sounds."

"It doesn't make it any less true," I replied, meeting his skeptical eyes.

"Go on," he said, his tone softening as curiosity

sparked in his voice. I could feel him leaning into the story, even if he wasn't entirely aware of it.

I chuckled, letting the memory take over. "You knocked on her door, and she thought you were some kind of villain. Being the responsible older sister, I snuck out the back door, came around to the front, and launched myself at you. I was going to take you down."

Zev's lips twitched, the barest hint of a smile breaking through his confusion. "And did you? Take me down, I mean?"

I laughed, shaking my head. "Not even close. You sidestepped my attack, and I flew right past you. Hit the porch so hard I almost rattled my brain loose. Iris came out thinking you'd flattened me, and she was ready to tear you apart. I had to convince her I'd done it to myself."

His laugh was low but genuine, and for a moment, it was like nothing had changed. "That sounds like an unforgettable encounter."

"Only, it was forgettable," I said, my voice quieter now. "You don't remember me. You don't remember any of it."

The lightness in his expression faded, but he surprised me by saying, "Tell me another story."

I arched an eyebrow, a teasing grin creeping onto my face. "Should I tell you about the time you threw yourself in front of a snotgurgle troll? Took a chest full of toxic mucus to save an archdruid you owed a debt to." I smiled. "The slate was wiped clean after that."

Zev gave me a look, somewhere between amused and intrigued. "Isn't their snot like acid?"

I snorted a laugh. "That you remember?"

"I have no idea how." He grinned and shook his head. "But yes."

I laughed. "I got hit with a load of snot right to the face, too. I had so much sympathy for the Wicked Witch after that because I was literally melting." I pantomimed dragging my hand down the side of my face. "It was the most painful thing I've ever experienced, and then it killed me."

"You were dead?" he asked, his voice skeptical but intrigued.

"For a hot minute," I said, the memory sharp and bittersweet. "Iris made a bargain with the goddess Macha to save us both. That's when Macha turned me into a half-giantess and turned you into a non-fire djinn."

"You're pretty short for a giantess."

"At the moment," I agreed.

"And I'm a fire djinn now?" he asked. "You said the goddess turned me into the non-fire kind. So which is it?"

"Yes." I sighed. This was another long story. I gave him the shortest version I could. "You gave up being a regular djinn to save my family. But it meant..." I hesitated, unsure if I should tell him everything. Did I mention that we'd been together? That I was the tall, dark-haired woman he had recalled loving? I shook my head. "It meant taking your fire back."

"I still don't know if I believe all this," he said, looking lost. "It's too incredible, but I remember some of the things you're talking about. Like the snotgurgle, for instance."

"But you don't remember fighting it?"

He shook his head. "No. Not that."

I took a step forward, and he tensed. What the hell was his problem? He let Veronica stand near him without treating her like a pariah. Why was he acting this way with me?

"Why are you keeping me at arm's length?" I asked.

"Because you're wrong," he said. "I don't know how, but you don't feel right."

"Because I feel wrong?"

He nodded.

"Fantastic." I glanced over at Carver. "Have you found anything yet?"

"Working on it," he said. "I found a couple of

spells that will take memory away, but none that will restore it."

"Maybe a hypnotist," Veronica suggested. "Don't they use them to help people uncover hidden trauma?"

"Do I have hidden trauma?" Zev asked.

Carver made a throaty noise, and I tapped my foot nervously.

"So, that would be a yes," Zev said.

"Let he who is without trauma go suck an egg," Veronica quipped. "We all have our stuff, dude. It's not a big deal."

I was sure Veronica had never had a lamia driving her body and using it for whatever her horrid mind could think of while her soul was trapped in a bottle, but I wasn't going to turn this into a trauma showdown.

Instead, I agreed. "Yep, everyone has stuff."

"Damn it," Carver said, tossing the book away from him. I'd never seen him treat his witch tools so carelessly.

I walked over and picked up the spell journal, handing it back to him. "Maybe we need to phone a friend."

"Who?" he asked.

"Someone who knows all about djinns and what might make them lose their memory."

"Ryker." He snapped to his feet and beelined to his phone. "Great idea."

"I have them every once in a while."

"Who's Ryker?" Veronica asked.

"A half-djinn we know," I told her. Ryker was so much more than that, she was an expert on the supernatural with a gift for reading magic. "She helped us find Zev."

Veronica's eyes widened. "He was lost?

"For seven months," I said.

Zev crossed his arms over his chest. "I was?"

"You'd been tricked and trapped in a djinn bottle," I explained. "We flew down to Mexico and saved you from a lamia."

"The snake goddess?" he asked.

"Well, I don't know if she was the goddess, but she sure acted the part." Watching the way, she'd manipulated Zev's body on stage had enraged me. It still did. "We just got you back yesterday."

Veronica wheezed and then coughed. "Inhaled my saliva," she rasped. "You just rescued this dude and got him home yesterday, and now your brother is missing?" She shook her head and cleared her throat again. "That's a lot of bad luck."

Carver gestured for me to come closer. "I got her," he said, putting the phone on speaker.

"Hey, Ryker," he greeted.

"Long time no see," the half-djinn djinnologist joked, considering we'd only parted the day before. "Don't tell me Zev's disappeared again."

"In a way," I said, stepping closer. "He went missing for about two hours today, and when he came back, his memory was wiped. He can remember some general knowledge stuff, but not anything related to his actual life."

"Aww, Mare," she said sympathetically. "That really sucks."

"On top of that, my brother Rowan was kidnapped by these guys who speak Gaulish, and we don't know why. We have no idea how to get him back."

"What do they want?" Ryker asked.

"Zev," I said.

"Oh." There was a pause. "Gotcha. More bad luck."

"Can you tell us what would cause a djinn to lose his memory?" Carver asked.

"As long as he has his power, I don't know how," Ryker replied. "I've never heard of it happening before, but ancient djinns didn't keep a written history. Most of the historical data is anecdotal or has been passed down by their masters."

"I was afraid of that," Carver said, running a hand through his hair.

I thought about how I'd lost the ability to wield fire since the transformation spell because I'd been changed at a cellular level. "What if the djinn had temporarily lost his magic?" I asked.

Ryker's voice sharpened. "How would that happen?"

"Carver brewed a transformation potion that changed us into other people. Regular mundane humans." With a slight resonation that his ring could pick up, but mostly regular. All our abilities had gone with the spell. "It was to keep our magic from triggering any alarms when we came to Eureka Springs early to see if we could find Rowan before the deadline."

"Holy squirrel nuts," Ryker swore. "Who thought that was a good idea?"

"All of us," I admitted, shouldering the blame. "We were desperate to find Rowan, and we needed disguises."

Ryker sighed. "Okay. How about I come down there and give Zev a once-over? Maybe I can figure it out. Being half-djinn, I can see things you might not be able to. You said he disappeared for a couple of hours?"

"Yes," I said. "With my car. When he returned, the car and both our phones were dead, and he no longer recognized us or himself."

"That's bad," Ryker said. "Really bad."

"How long will it take you to get here?" I asked, stifling a yawn. The lack of sleep was catching up with me.

"It'll take me about an hour to put together a flight plan for Hammer Field. It's closed, but I know a guy who knows a guy. It's about six miles outside Eureka Springs."

"I know where it is," Veronica said. "Near the Cadet Aviation Museum."

"Who's that?" Ryker asked.

"New friend," I told her. "She's a kitchen witch."

"Cool-cool," Ryker said. "Once I get my flight plan registered, I'll head down. Should get there before one-thirty."

"That would be great," I said. "We could use the help."

"I'll need a ride once I land. The old airstrip doesn't have a car rental place."

"I'll come get you," Veronica offered.

"I'll go with her," Carver added.

"It's a plan!" Ryker enthused. "See you in a few hours."

After we got off the phone, I sagged into the loveseat. I forced myself to stand and went to the bureau where Carver had plugged in mine and Zev's phone. I tried turning mine on and it was exactly what I feared. Whatever had happened to Zev, my car, and these phones, had killed them dead.

"If we can't find Rowan by tonight, I'm going to need a new phone."

"If you need to have a phone, they got a twenty-four-hour Walmart in Berryville. I can run you over later. Swap out the sim card, and voila. No harm, no foul."

So far, everything about this day had been foul. I grabbed the phones and tucked them in my purse. "I'm going to need a power nap before Ryker gets here," I told them. "My whole body feels like I'm carrying around sandbags."

"Good idea," Carver said, scrubbing his hands over his face. "We could all use a nap."

"I'm good," Veronica told us. "You three nap. I'll call a tow truck for Marigold's car and go gas up mine."

"Really?" I gave her a grateful look. "That would be awesome."

She smiled. "I have my moments."

Zev shifted, looking slightly uncertain. "Where is my room?"

"You're sharing with Carver," I told him, too tired to explain why my room was his room. I nodded toward Carver. "Wake me when Ryker gets here."

Carver nodded as I pushed myself off the

loveseat and shuffled toward my room. The weight of the past day settled heavier on me, but Ryker was an ally, and she knew the ins and outs of the supernatural world as much as Zev and maybe more than Carver. For the first time since this mess began, I felt a sliver of hope.

Chapter Eleven

I WAS RELIEVED THAT RYKER WAS COMING. After spending two days in the trenches at Natheria with the monster-hunting half-djinn, I trusted her with my life. More than that, I trusted her with Zev's. Ryker had the ability to read and identify magic. Aside from a long life, it was one of the rare djinn qualities she'd inherited from her father, a powerful marid djinn.

I'd seen her work up close. She'd read my aura when we met and accurately pegged me as half-giant with a pinch of witch and something else. That something else, it turned out, was ifrit. I'd become a sebtusiptu, which basically meant a soul token, for Zev, thanks to my spell gone awry. If anyone had a chance of figuring out what had been done to Zev, it was Ryker.

She'd also warned me that if anyone found out I was a walking, talking sebtusiptu, it would put me in great danger. If someone wanted to, they could use me to control Zev. Was that what was happening here? Was the person behind the kidnapping after both of us? That still didn't explain Zev's short disappearance or his amnesia.

My head hurt thinking about it. There were so many pieces of the puzzle missing. I was mentally, physically, and emotionally wiped out, and I couldn't focus on all the awfulness for another second. After a quick shower, I let it all go and crashed hard. I woke up a little over two hours later to a loud, consistent knock on the door.

"Marigold," Carver said through the door. "Come on, wake up."

I wiped dried spittle from the corner of my mouth and where it had crusted on my cheek. Yuck. I didn't normally drool in my sleep, but that's how worn out I'd been. I decided to blame it on Nikky. I was in her body, after all. I sluggishly forced myself to sit up and dangle my short legs off the side of the bed.

I looked in the mirror on the opposite wall and scowled. "You're still here, huh?" I was beginning to despise Nikky. Carver had said the spell would last twelve to twenty-four hours. We'd drunk the potion nearly eight hours earlier, which meant we still had at least another four hours together.

My grayscale vision added to the gloom and doom. I'd jumped in headfirst and with both feet when Carver suggested the potion, even after he'd laid out the side effects. Still, rational or not, I was kind of mad at him. He hadn't warned us that Zev would lose his magic. Maybe he hadn't known, but I got the sense that even if he had, he would've pushed for us to use it. He was desperate to find Rowan. That was the one thing I couldn't be mad about.

Even so, whatever had happened to Zev during those missing hours, he'd been defenseless to stop because of the spell. The thought nauseated me.

"Marigold!" Carver said more sharply. "Ryker's here. She and Veronica brought food."

I groaned as I got to my feet. "I'm up," I groused back. "Give me two minutes to brush my teeth and run a comb over my hair." I knew my body needed fuel, but the scone I'd eaten earlier had been less than appetizing. Without a sense of smell, I could taste that it had been sweet and crumbly, but other than that, it had been flavorless.

My stomach growled in protest to my ambivalence.

"Fine," he huffed. "Two minutes."

I scrubbed my face and walked to a window

overlooking the street below. True to her word, Veronica had called for a tow on my car. At least, I hoped she had, considering it was no longer in the yellow zone. Once we rescued Rowan, I would make him reimburse me for all the pain and suffering. It was a joke. Not the pain and suffering part, because that was all too real, but I would happily go bankrupt if it meant having my brother home safe and sound.

I felt bad that I'd put my nose in it with Carver. He and Rowan deserved privacy to figure out their relationship without busybody sisters interfering. Rowan had never been married, and I didn't think he'd ever brought any of his dates home to meet us or our parents. There were times I thought he might be asexual, which would've been all right by me as well. He was Ro, my big brother, and I would love him, whoever that happened to be. I'd only gotten an inkling that he might be gay or bisexual because I'd spent seven months watching the sparks between him and Carver during our lessons.

Even so, a part of me thought it might be wishful thinking. I'd been lonely without Zev, so I hadn't wanted my brother to be alone. But he wasn't me. For all I knew, he could've been perfectly content without a partner. I mean, I had been for many years before I met the fiery ifrit who turned my heart upside down.

Whatever was happening, Rowan could tell me or not tell me in his own good time. I made a mental note to apologize to Carver as well. Ugh. The nap had given me a semi-fresh brain with too much time to go over everything I might have said wrong to make my friend unhappy.

"Stop spiraling," I told myself. A white SUV caught my attention as it drove past the hotel and turned right on Center Street. Was it a coincidence? I'd read once that white was the cheapest vehicle color, which is why cars and trucks painted white were cheaper to buy. That meant there were an awful lot of them on the road. The SUV circled around and drove past the hotel again, only going south this time.

I watched for another minute, and the vehicle didn't come back. Still, I made a note to tell Carver before I got distracted. I cleaned up in the bathroom, put on some deodorant, and brushed my teeth. I grabbed my keycard and my purse, then headed to Carver's suite.

Ryker's bright purple hair looked silver with my black-and-white vision as she stood outside the door waiting for me. I hugged her hard. "Thank you for coming."

"Wow," she said. "Damn, Marigold. You look like you're playing hooky from the North Pole." Ryker was sixty-eight years old but didn't look a day over seventeen. She had clear, smooth, light brown skin, dark expressive eyes that were slightly wide, making them even more striking, a sharp, small nose, and high cheekbones. Even in monochrome, the woman was stunning.

I leaned my head back. "Yes, I'm tiny. And from what I hear, this outfit has a lot of green in it. If you got more elf jokes, tell them later."

"Dang, girl." She rubbed the shaved side of her head. "It really is you." She was taller than me by half a foot. She wore dark cargo pants, black combat boots, and a black The Slits t-shirt.

"Have you had a chance to check out Zev yet?" I asked.

She grimaced. "That's why I'm out here talking to you. I can sense a bandish on him, but I can't find it."

"What's a bandish?"

Ryker rocked back on her heels, using hand gestures as she explained. "It's a binding hex, or more accurately, in Zev's case, I think someone or something cast a sealing curse on him."

"For what purpose?"

She gave me a "duh" look. "To capture him," she said. "Like the lamia had. It's a spell used to reduce a djinn to smoke so they can be trapped."

"But he's not smoke."

"Exactly. Whoever set the spell is probably wondering what they did wrong." Her expression pinched. "Still, I couldn't find the mark." She moved her hands with a flourish as she continued, "With a bandish, there's a sigil that focuses the sealing. It can be transferred with a handshake, a pat on the back, or someone clasping your arm. Anywhere the person doing the hexing can easily transfer the curse to the djinn's skin. Of course, I haven't checked every inch of his body, but I can't imagine it's in any of his nooks and crannies."

The hall was a little cool, so I crossed my arms over my chest and tucked in my hands for warmth. "How can we know for sure he has this mark on him? Is it visible to the naked eye?" I'd make the ifrit, no matter how reluctant, strip down to his birthday suit if that's what it took.

Ryker shook her head. "It's invisible. But I can see them." She bit her lower lip.

"But...?" I hated when people dragged out bad news. "Just say it."

"But djinns, especially one as old and smart as Zev, would know how to protect themselves from this kind of sealing."

"Zev's powers have been suppressed under the

transformation spell," I told her, surprised Carver hadn't already mentioned it.

"No wonder," Ryker said. "I was freaking out that his ifrit magic was nearly non-existent. Even after you freed him from the lamia, and his power had been weakened, he was saturated with the magic of the djinn. I was worried something the lamia did had weakened him even more."

I shook my head. "Nope. This was all our doing."

"This is why he had no defense against the bandish. He isn't a djinn at the moment, which is why he isn't a wisp of smoke in a jug somewhere. The curse isn't working the way it was intended."

"The transformation potion is temporary." I stared up at her, meeting her dark gaze. "When it stops working, will the bandish start working?"

She ugly-faced grimaced at my suggestion. "It's possible. The spell is strong, but it's buried. Transforming back into an ifrit could unbury it."

The door opened. "You coming in?" Carver said. "Burgers are getting cold."

We went inside. Veronica greeted me while shoving a fry in her mouth. Zev gave me a slight nod but still kept his distance. He had a half-eaten burger on the end table near him.

"Not hungry?" I asked, taking one of the

wrapped burgers from a bag, along with a small sack of fries, and sitting in one of the wingback chairs.

"Everything tastes like ash," he said.

I unwrapped the thick, juicy burger with a thick tomato, bacon, cheese, and avocado—all in various shades of gray. So appetizing, not. "You might as well have grabbed burgers from McDonald's," I said, taking a bite. It tasted a little salty with sour notes, but little else. "When food is flavorless, all the joy is taken out of eating."

Veronica waved her sandwich at Carver. "Hey, if we could modify that spell of yours only to affect the nose, you could probably bottle that shit and sell it as a new weight-loss supplement." She giggled. "We'd rake in the big bucks."

"Uhm, yeah, no," Carver said, scarfing down a fry. "I wouldn't wish this on my worst enemy."

I gave him a sly look.

He laughed. "Okay, maybe on my worst enemy."

"Unfortunately, we haven't eaten in the past twenty-four hours, and Mamma needs fuel," I said. "Even if that fuel tastes like ass?"

"You can taste ass?" Ryker teased. "That's a flavor."

"You're an ass," I said, taking another bite to cover my grin.

"Oh, I see," Veronica mused. "You flirt with everyone."

"I'm not flirting with you," I shot back.

She laughed. "Okay, miss sassy-pants."

I shook my head. I glanced over at Zev. He was so quiet and withdrawn. He didn't look like the man I loved, and he wasn't acting like him either. And what happened once the potion wore off? If his being an ifrit triggered the hex that had caused his amnesia, then we'd lose him all over again.

Not on my watch. "We need to find the bandish and remove it before he changes back into an ifrit," I said.

"Whoa," Veronica said. "Okay, down to business."

I set my burger down and walked over to where Zev sat.

"Don't come any closer."

I stopped a few feet from him.

He turned his knees away from me, but he didn't get up. "Can you take another step back?"

I did as he asked. "What makes you so uncomfortable whenever I get near you?" I rubbed my thumb against the side of my index finger to keep myself calm. "I mean, what are your symptoms? Objective or subjective?"

"Objectively," he said, "it feels like pins and

needles over my chest and upper back. The closer you get, the more active it gets. But it's more an intense sensation than pain."

I nodded. "Anything else?"

"My hands get warm. Again, not painful, but it doesn't feel right."

"Wrong," I repeated what he'd said about me earlier. "It feels wrong."

"Yes," he stated.

"And subjectively?"

"Your proximity causes some kind of revulsion in my body. Like I need to get away from you. No..." He shook his head. "I have to get away."

"But when I'm not close?"

"It goes away."

I turned to Ryker. "Well, babe. What do you think?"

She paced for a moment, mumbling to herself, then asked Zev, "Do you think you could hold still long enough for Marigold to touch your arm?"

His face reflected mild panic. "I don't know."

"I want to see if the magic I felt when I checked you out earlier changes when she's in contact, but if you can't—"

"I'll do it," he cut her off, his voice strained. "You can tie me down if that's what it takes."

137

"Are you sure?" I asked, taking a step toward him again.

He got up from his seat. "Not when you're close, I'm not, but I know the feeling isn't real. There's a part of me that knows you are my friend."

Ouch. I mean, yes, I was glad he thought I might be a friend, but we were so much more. I was his soulmate. Literally.

I forced a smile. "I am," I told him. "I would never do anything that I thought would hurt you."

"Fine, then," he said. "You might have to tie me down."

"That's what she said," Carver said flatly.

I pivoted my gaze to him and chuckled. "Time and place, man. So not appropriate."

It got a smile from Zev, though, so there was that.

Veronica wiggled her eyebrows. "Who packed the handcuffs?"

I groaned and gave Zev an apologetic glance. "It's not too late to change your mind."

His smile faded. "Yes, it is."

He was right. Time wasn't on our side. It hadn't been since this whole thing began. Time was running out for Zev and Rowan, and I would lose them unless I could figure out how to fix both situations.

I stared past Zev to the window and grinned

sheepishly. Thick braided cords held the curtains aside. "I found some rope." I pointed to the curtains and then looked at Zev. "Let's get you strapped down."

He gave me a lopsided smile that for a moment reminded me of the man he'd forgotten. "I bet you've been wanting to do that for a while."

That was unexpectedly flirty. I laughed. "What makes you think I already haven't?"

His eyes widened, and I laughed again. It was either laugh or cry, and crying wouldn't help a damn thing.

Chapter Twelve

ZEV STOOD IN THE MIDDLE OF THE ROOM, HIS jaw tight, his arms crossed over his chest as Ryker gave her instructions. "Strip down to your underwear," she said, her tone clinical and unbothered, like she was a doctor giving a routine order.

He hesitated, glancing at me from the corner of his eye, then back to her. "Seriously?"

"Seriously," she replied, unfazed. "I need to see how your skin reacts when Marigold gets close. If there's a shift or a flare, we'll miss it with all those layers in the way."

"Oh, yeah." Veronica rubbed her hands together. "Dinner *and* a show."

"Not helpful," I told her.

"My bad," she said, but she looked far from remorseful.

Zev huffed out a breath, muttering something under it that sounded like, "This better work." Quickly, like ripping off a Band-Aid, he stripped his shirt off, yanking it over his head and tossing it onto the chair. His jeans came next, pooling at his feet before he kicked them aside, leaving him in dark boxer briefs that clung to his lean form.

"Some mood music would've taken that striptease to a ten," Veronica commented.

Carver narrowed his gaze on her. "Don't make me put you in time out. Think about if the roles were reversed how that would make you feel."

She sobered quickly. "You're right. My bad."

Zev's narrowed brow and deep scowl wasn't hard to read. The man was not amused by any of what was happening.

I kept my gaze as neutral as possible. Objectively speaking, his body was... fine. More than fine. Lean, with sharp angles at his hips and a long torso that reminded me of those newer actors gracing movie posters everywhere. Timothy Chalamet came to mind—fine-boned and charming in a way that appealed to younger women.

But this Zev in front of me...well, he wasn't *my* Zev. This body lacked the rugged edges I missed so much. The strength and solidness that made me feel safe when he pulled me into his arms. It hadn't even been a full day, and I already ached for him like a missing limb. This version of him didn't make me feel anything but loss.

"On the bed," Ryker ordered him, snapping me out of my thoughts.

Zev climbed onto the bed stiffly, lying on his back, his arms at his sides. Carver stepped forward, holding one of the curtain cords. "I swear this feels like something out of a bad BDSM movie," he muttered, looping the cord around Zev's wrist and tying it to the headboard.

"Carver," I said, rolling my eyes. "Do we really want to encourage her?" I jerked my thumb at the kitchen witch.

"Good point," he said.

Veronica grinned as she worked on Zev's other wrist. "I don't take much encouragement, Marigold."

I rolled my eyes. "I've noticed." I gave her a "this is serious" stare.

In response, she wiggled her eyebrows at me. The girl was so unserious. On a good day, I would have loved her for it. This wasn't a good day.

Zev, for his part, ignored the banter entirely, staring up at the ceiling as if we weren't tying him up like a scene out of a 40s horror movie.

Once he was secure, Ryker stepped back to

inspect the knots. "Okay. That should hold if he starts thrashing. Marigold, you're up."

I swallowed hard, praying silently to the goddess that this would work and not somehow make everything worse.

Ryker's gaze met mine, steady with intent. "We're going slow," she said. "Ease your way over to him. I want to watch the magic and see how it reacts."

"Got it," I said, exhaling slowly. As I took my first hesitant step toward the bed, a line from Edgar Allan Poe's *The Pit and the Pendulum* popped into my head and refused to leave: *Inch by inch, line by line.* It played on repeat as I moved closer.

Zev's body remained still, but I could see the tension in his arms and shoulders as I approached. I couldn't tell if it was the binding spell or just me, but the air between us felt heavy, like a storm was about to break. With every step, I focused on Ryker out of the corner of my eye, watching as she scanned Zev's body for any changes.

"Keep going," Ryker said softly.

I nodded and stepped closer. My hands fidgeted at my sides, itching to reach out and touch him, to reassure myself that he was still there, still real. But the closer I got, the more his body seemed to react—

not visibly, but I could feel the resistance, like an invisible wall pressing back against me.

"Stop," Ryker said suddenly, her hand lifting to signal. "That's close enough for now."

I froze mid-step, my heart pounding. "What do you see?" I asked, my voice low.

Her eyes narrowed as she leaned closer, her hands moving in slow, deliberate patterns as she studied the space around him. "There's definitely something there," she murmured. "The magic's reacting to her proximity, but... it's not flaring the way I expected."

"Good or bad?" I asked, not sure if I wanted the answer.

She looked up at me, her expression unreadable. "Too early to say. But don't move just yet. Let's see what happens when you stay here for a moment longer."

I clenched my fists, digging my nails into my palms to keep steady. Zev's eyes were closed now, his jaw tight, but I couldn't tell if it was pain, frustration, or something else entirely.

The skin on Zev's torso stretched taut over his ribs, the shadows and curves of his lean frame more pronounced than ever. Then I saw it—a circular pattern emerging just under his sternum. I froze. I'd seen it before: an oval beneath an upside-down triangle, with two shapes like devil horns jutting out on either side.

"Do you see that?" I asked, my voice hushed.

"I do," Ryker said, her gaze fixed on the sigil. "It's still fuzzy, though. The magic, I mean. I'm going to need you to touch it."

Before I could process her words, a raw, guttural bellow ripped from Zev's throat. "Nooo! Get away from me!" His voice was animalistic, desperate. His eyes, wild and filled with panic, locked onto me like I was a threat. He thrashed against the curtain cords, his arms pulling so hard that the entire four-poster bed shook under his efforts.

"Zev!" I shouted, stepping back instinctively. "Stop! You're hurting yourself."

But he wasn't listening. He pulled harder, his body arching as if he could rip free through sheer force of will. The cords creaked and groaned, digging into his wrists and ankles.

Ryker's voice cut through the chaos, sharp and unyielding. "Don't hesitate, Marigold. Make contact with the sigil. We need to bring it all the way to the surface."

My stomach churned at the sight of him—his face twisted in excruciating pain, his entire body fighting as if his life depended on it. I felt physically ill. This was the last thing I wanted. I never wanted to hurt him. Not like this.

"Ryker," I said, my voice trembling. "I don't think—"

"Do it!" she barked, her tone leaving no room for argument. "It's the only way!"

I looked at Zev, my heart breaking at the agony in his eyes. I took a deep breath, pushing down the guilt and fear clawing at my chest. He wasn't going to like this. Hell, I didn't like this. But if there was even a chance it could help him, I had no choice.

Inch by inch, line by line, I stepped forward and reached out. My hand hovered just above the sigil, trembling. "Zev," I whispered, my voice shaking. "I'm so sorry." Then I pressed my palm to the mark.

"Stop. This isn't me," he gritted out through clenched teeth. His cheeks flexed, his jaw tightened, and he turned his face away from me, his eyes squeezed shut. "Please stop."

"It's too much," I said to Ryker, my voice cracking. "We're making it worse."

"Keep your hand on it," she ordered, her voice firm and steady as her hands moved above mine. "I'm getting something now. I've just about got it."

Zev's body writhed beneath my touch, but I pressed harder, grounding myself in his struggle. My hand burned with a bright and searing pain, forcing me to yank my hand back. Colors had never looked so vibrant. The scent of musty hotel was a feast for my nose. On my palm was Zev's symbols. The pointy triangles, marking me as he *sebtusiptu* had returned. And my hands, there were no longer pale and petite. My palms were wide, my fingers long and strong. The hair that cascaded over my shoulder was straight and dark as pitch. Thank the goddess, the tunic and leggings were stretchy, or I would've gone She-Hulk and tore them apart at the seams.

"I'm back," I said, simultaneously elated and worried. If Zev changed before Ryker could deactivate the bandish, he'd be bound and sealed away.

I squeezed my hand, my nails digging deeply into my palm until they bled. I called on the strength of my forest giant ancestry and the power of Zev's fire, and I slammed my hand down over the sigil once more.

The cry from Zev struck at something in my core, something I didn't know I could tap into. It was the soul fragment. Zev might not know himself, but his soul did, and it took over.

"You are Zevian Diabreesa Ma'ham," I intoned, my voice low and commanding. "Formerly Za'fir of Mesopotamia. You are a powerful and magnificent ifrit who has walked this earth for several millennia.

You are more than this pain, more than this cage, and more than this curse."

Ryker leaned closer, her fingers tracing the air above my hand as if pulling invisible threads. "I'm close," I heard her mutter, but the voice of Zev's soul fragment wasn't done.

It continued to call out to Zev. "You are the Flamebringer of ancient sands, the Ashbearer of the Red Desert, the Unbroken Inferno who stood against the Seven Masters of Pylian'tor. You are not bound, Zev. You cannot be bound. This is not who you are."

Zev's breathing hitched, a guttural noise ripping from his throat. His eyes flew open, blazing with the faintest flicker of fire, as if something deep inside him was waking. His eyes went from ice blue to the deepest shade of whiskey brown, flames licking from his pupils. The cords holding him to the bed shuddered, vibrating like plucked strings.

"He's transforming back...but the sigil. It's still there. I can feel it under my palm."

Ryker nodded sharply. "I'm struggling to undo the bandish. This one has so many intricate knots and branches and dead ends like a maze. I keep having to start over." Her face was pinched with worry. "I don't know if I can get it done in time."

This wasn't the end. I wouldn't let it be. I increased the pressure on his stomach, feeling the heat of the triangles beneath my palm like a live ember. "Zev," I said, my voice softer now, steady despite the storm of emotions raging inside me. "You're not alone. Fight this. Come back to me. Please."

His wild eyes met mine, and for a moment, I thought I saw recognition—a spark of the man I loved fighting through the haze.

Blood, I heard a voice in my head said. *Our blood to his blood. His blood to ours.*

"Carver," I shouted. "Give me your knife. Hurry."

He hurried to his case and took out the silver athame and held it out to me. "What are you going to do."

His sandy brown hair had started to turn black, and his jaw widened, his lips full and wide. His hair was already turning to wisps of smoke. I was losing him. Goddess, don't let it be too late.

"No. Not this time," I said out loud. I took the knife from Carver and sliced across my palm, then I used the tip to pierce the pulsing sigil on his stomach. He didn't cry out in pain this time, but I could feel down to the cell the horrific agony he experienced. I pressed my bloodied hand to his open wound. I repeated what the voice in my head had said. "Our blood to your blood. Your blood to our blood."

The sigil burst into flames under my hand. I moved it away and watched as the oval, triangle, and horns burned from his flesh until there was nothing remaining but a raw third-degree burn.

Zev's eyes widened as the rest of the transformation spell reverted, and he was again my gorgeous, beautiful man. Solid and one-hundred percent smoke free.

Elation roared through me. My head snapped back, and flames tore from my throat into the air.

"She's going to burn the place down," I heard Veronica shout.

"Get the fire extinguisher," Ryker added.

The flame kept coming as if I was vomiting out days of trauma and terror in a fiery celebration that threatened to kill us all. I knew it was bad but I couldn't stop myself.

And then I felt strong arms wrap around me, his lips crushing against mine, his kiss drinking down my fire, like he was trying to tether us together with the flame. My eyes flashed open, and I no longer saw a desperate man who didn't know who or what he was. This man was completely in control, and his gaze wasn't worried or full of doubt. No, his gaze said, *You are mine.* His hands gripped my arms, hard enough to bruise, but I didn't pull away.

Instead, I poured everything I had into him—my magic, my strength, my love.

The heat between us flared, and I could feel the push and pull of his ifrit magic tangling with mine. It wasn't smooth or gentle—raw and jagged, like a wild-fire licking at my skin. My body responded instinctively, my own magic rising to meet his.

A sound fire extinguisher spray stopped us cold. What little residue landed on us was superficial. I blinked, my lips still on Zev's. He was grinning like a man who was far from finished.

"My key is on the dresser," I muttered through the press. "Take it and go."

When nobody moved. Zev growled. "Out!"

When the door slammed shut behind him, he said, "You have on too many clothes, *libbu sa*."

I grinned as he stripped the tunic top over my head, then squealed when he lifted me up and flipped me onto my back. He crawled on top of me, his knees settling between my thighs. He lifted one of my hands and looped it into the curtain cord.

"What are you doing?" I asked suspiciously.

"Turnabout is fair, no?" His eyes glittered with devilish intent. "You tied me up. Now it's my turn."

"Uhm, point of order." I reached down with my free hand and cupped his thick erection. "I, in fact, did not participate in tying you up."

His smile widened, and he flashed me his pearly whites. "How does that popular phrase go?" He looked up to the left as if trying to recall it then turned his gaze back to mine. "Snooze, you lose." He tied my other hand.

"Actually, it's 'you snooze, you lose.' However, I don't see any losers here."

He traced a finger along my collarbone, sending a shiver down my spine, his amber eyes glinting like liquid fire.

Breathless, I said, "God, I've missed you."

His mouth tilted into a smirk, his lips brushing against the shell of my ear. "You mean *this*?" he asked, his fingers sliding between my thighs, coaxing a shudder from me. "Or do you mean *me*?"

I soft guttural moan escaped my lips as his expert fingers went to work. "Yes, this. You. All of it." The pleasure began to build overwhelming my senses as I gave into it.

"Good," he said, his voice dropping to a husky whisper as his lips traced the line of my jaw. "Because you have me. Every inch."

His words sent a flush racing through me, and I could feel his grin against my skin as he worked my leggings down my legs, his hands slow and deliberate, teasing and reverent all at once.

"Thank you, my love," he whispered against my skin.

"For what?"

"For bringing me back."

"Always," I whispered. "I will always come for you. I will always bring you back to me. You're mine as much as I am yours."

"I am yours," he agreed. "Body, mind, and soul." A blaze of heat flickered in his gaze as he kissed my breasts and my stomach, going down until his shoulders were between my knees. "And I plan to prove it in every way."

And prove it he did, his touch ignited a fire in me that burned away the fear, the pain, and the lingering shadows of doubt. In that moment, there was nothing but us—our magic, our love, and the certainty that no matter what storms came our way, we would always find our way back to each other.

Chapter Thirteen

AFTER PLAYING A LITTLE, YOU SCRUB MY BACK, and I'll scrub yours in the shower, we stole the two complimentary robes in Carver's bathroom, then went down the hall to our suite. Carver's transformation spell hadn't ended when mine and Zev's did, so he still looked like Gym Bro Archie.

"Well, well, well," Veronica said as we entered the room. "This is the hottest walk of shame I've ever seen."

"We, uhm, had a few things to discuss," I said to no one in particular.

"We heard," Ryker stated.

"The whole sixth floor heard," Carver added. "It was a very loud conversation."

"There were a lot of 'oh, gods, oh yeses,' so I have to give the dialogue a C, but the robust way you two made your point was A plus-plus." Veronica gave a chef's kiss off her fingertips and winked.

I groaned. "You can go back to the other room now," I told them. "We need to get dressed."

"Ah, hell no." Carver shook his head, picked up our bags, and tossed them to us. "You wrecked it. You bought it."

Ryker and Veronica laughed.

I tried not to, but I joined in. It was a necessary moment of respite. When the giggling fits finally stopped, Veronica thrust her hand out to Zev. "I'm Veronica," she said. "Nice to meet you."

He arched a brow at her. "You do realize we've already met."

"But you had..." She shook her hands at him. "You couldn't remember anything."

"My memory has returned," he said. "Including the memories of when I had amnesia, with the exception of what caused my amnesia in the first place."

Ryker snorted. "Give the girl a break. You don't look like you did half an hour ago."

Veronica smiled. "Yeah, sorry." She eyeballed me up and down. "You really are a tall drink of water. Damn, girl." She sighed. "I see it now." She glanced between Zev and me. "Electric."

I shook my head and raised a brow. "Fire."

"Sizzle." She licked her thumb and pressed it to

her ass. "Scorching hot." She shook her head. "I'm a witch, so I'm not new to magic, but I'm willing to admit that I've never seen anything like that before."

"As much fun as it is to discuss Marigold and Zev's sex life," Carver interjected, "it's time we start planning how we're going to save Rowan from the Treehouse thugs."

"My powers have fully returned," Zev said. "I can apparate into the cabin and take him out with me."

"Oh, really?" I glared at Zev. "You just going to pop in and out, huh?"

He spread his hands. "And why not?"

My brain immediately started playing through everything that could and probably would go wrong. "For one, these jackholes have gone out of their way to lure you down here on a specific day, and they have been here for how long? Days? Weeks? Who knows!" I threw up my hands and my robe split open.

Zev let out a low catcall whistle, and I hastily closed the gap.

"My point is, they knew you would be coming, and for all we know, they believed you'd be at full power to begin with. You don't think they won't be prepared for you? I bet they have djinn traps, or whatever, in every single one of these cabins. On top of that, we don't even know what cabin they're holding Rowan in or if he's even out there. That place could be a red herring. I saw one of their white SUVs driving past the hotel twice earlier. This could all be one elaborate trap."

Zev put his arm around me. "You have made your point, *libbu sa*."

I leaned my head against his shoulder. "I certainly freaking hope so."

"Wait." Carver held up his hand. "Did you say you saw a white SUV circling the block?"

"Yes, I was going to tell you earlier and then...well, you know. Stuff happens."

"Squirrel," he said.

"Exactly. I got a little distracted."

"It wasn't little," Zev deadpanned.

I stared at him for a moment, then barked a laugh. "You're hilarious."

"And big," he added.

I belly laughed then. "Stop. You're killing me." But I loved his humor and his confidence. They were two out of the three things that made him extremely attractive. The third, of course, was his heart. He was stunning on the outside, but his insides eclipsed that beauty. And, of course, bringing up a close fourth was his big dick. Let's just say, he had every right to be proud. This was the first time he'd acted like his old self since we got him out of Natheria, and it made my soul—and his—happy.

"As fun as all this innuendo is, back to the big picture," Carver said.

We all groaned.

"What?" he asked, confused, then his eyes widened, and he shook his head. "You all know what I mean."

"We do," I told him. "Getting Rowan back safe and sound is the number one priority."

"I think our first priority should be finding out what happened to Zev when he disappeared," Ryker said. "It may not be related, but we have to look at all the available information."

Zev's expression darkened. "I was texting with my contact, and I was transported with the car to a secluded island somewhere."

"Wait. What? My car? You were transported in my car?"

He nodded. "It's a blank from that moment until I found myself in the car without my memories."

When I was overwhelmed, I had trouble recalling small details sometimes, and I remembered that when Ryker was working on bringing the bandish hex to the surface, it was shaped just like the tattoo on the hulking dude at the Grand Treehouse Resort who'd threatened to batter us.

"It's definitely connected," I told them. "Zev's hex and the guy from the resort were the same symbol."

"Describe it," Ryker said.

I got a pencil and pad out of the hotel desk drawer and drew the symbol. "See." I pointed at the drawing. "It's an oval with an upside-down triangle and little horns."

Ryker looked at Zev.

He shook his head. "I'm unfamiliar with it."

"Same," she said. "That worries me."

"Since this happened when you were texting your contact, do you think they set you up?" I asked.

He shook his head. "No, I don't believe they would do so."

Hmmmm, still not using any pronouns. Cagey AF. "Because you trust her?"

He gave me a sharp look. "I wouldn't go that far. But I also don't think she would set me up to be bandished."

"Okay, Zev," Ryker said. "Spill. Who's your contact, and what were you contacting her about?"

Right. Ryker didn't know about the recording. "Rowan had gotten the man who kidnapped him recorded saying some phrases that sounded Gaulish. Zev has a contact who could translate."

"Yeah, dude," Ryker stated with an eye roll. "Me."

"You speak Gaulish?" Carver asked incredulously.

"I speak about twenty different dead languages." She gave him a *WTF* look.

"How long have we known each other?" He looked only mildly upset. "How do I not know this? I mean, I knew you spoke Akkadian, but twenty dead languages?"

Ryker shrugged. "I guess it never came up."

"It's coming up now," I told them. I waved my hand in a slight flourish at Carver. "You guys go get the recorder." I was becoming acutely aware of my nakedness under the robe when a slight breeze from the wall unit slipped under the hem. "While you do that, I can get dressed."

"I will stay with you," Zev said.

"Damn right you will," I told him. "Naked, you are a walking fire hazard."

"I love a fiery woman," he smirked.

"That fiery woman better only be me, or I'll fry your dick into next Tuesday," I said as we took our bags into the bathroom and shut the door.

Zev shrugged. "It'll grow back." He took me in his arms and let his eyes go a little sleepy and seductive. "And it will grow back twice as big."

"Oh, Lord." I swallowed a nervous laugh. "No, thanks. We're good. Any bigger, and I would have to buy a wagon to haul it around." If he thought all this sexy talk was going to get him a get-out-of-jail-free card, he was sorely mistaken.

He raised a brow. "It's my sister."

"Who?" My brain picked that moment to stop computing, but, in the end, it put two and two together. "Your contact?"

He inclined his head. "We have a... difficult relationship. Complicated."

"But she knows Gaulish?"

"She spent many years there." He pressed his forehead to mine. "I betrayed her confidence, and she's never forgiven me."

"She was your source, wasn't she? The one who told you the Gauls' escape routes."

He nodded. "She didn't know that I planned to tell Caesar. How could she?"

"Did she have a master in Gaul? Is that why she was there?"

Zev closed his eyes. "She was in love with a Helvetii warrior who worked closely with Divico, the leader of the Helvetii."

"Oh, Zev." His guilt had been doubly compounded. "What happened to her lover?"

"He was killed during the Battle of Bibracte."

I wanted to believe his sister wouldn't set him up to be captured, but love could make you do crazy things. It had been over two thousand years, though. Maybe she'd moved on. "When was the last time you talked to her?"

"A hundred and seven years ago," he replied.

"And?"

"She was cordial and friendly, but we'd been close when we were young. That closeness no longer exists."

"That sucks." I had three sisters and a brother, all of us adopted, and I didn't know what I'd do if any of them stayed mad at me for a day, let alone two millennia. "I'm sorry."

"It is what it is." He slid his hands inside my robe, the heat of his fingers as they slipped down my back to rest on my ass. "This makes it better."

"My ass?" I chuckled.

"My ass," he said, then shook his head and smiled. "You, Iris, your siblings, even your nephew Michael and your father. You have given me a home, Marigold Everlee. You have given me back a family. I will never take that for granted." He kissed me, his lips tender against mine. "It's why I would trade myself for your brother. I would do anything for you. For your kin."

And he had. He'd given up everything to save my

father, and he had more than proven he would do it again if it meant saving Rowan.

"I would do the same for you," I told him. "I hope you know just how soul-crushingly in love I am with you."

He tapped the side of my head before pulling me close into a tight embrace. "Everything you feel, I feel as well. I never believed there was such a thing as this kind of love. It's why I barely hesitated when I betrayed Kah'ar. I thought she would get over it. That love was lust disguised as emotion, and she would move on to someone else."

"And now?"

"If she felt an ounce of what I feel for you, then I am eternally shamed for what I took from her. The fact that she could go on living after is a testament to her strength." He took one hand out of my robe and stroked my hair. "If anything happened to you, I would find a way to die. Or stop living if dying wasn't possible. You are my penance and my redemption."

I fought back the tears, taking his face in both my hands and kissing him soundly. "Samsies."

He chuckled then reluctantly let me go. "We should get dressed, unless you want to have another...conversation."

"I want to conversate with you all the time," I said.

He moved in close again, just as Carver knocked on the door. "Hurry up. Ryker has translated the Gaulish."

Zev shook his head. "I guess our conversation will have to wait until later."

"When this is over, we're going to spend a week doing nothing but talking."

His brow dipped. "We are still talking about sex, right?"

I giggled. "Absolutely."

"Good. Just checking." He kissed me one more. "I'm not ready for the others to know about my sister. Can we keep that between us for now?"

"Okay," I said. "But what if she's involved?"

"Then we will tell them. Knowing or not knowing about her won't change whatever is to come." He ran his thumb over my bottom lip. "Trust me, *libbu sa*. Kah'ar wouldn't betray me like this."

I wanted to believe him, but there was a lot of water under that bridge between them. Even so, I said, "I'll keep it to myself."

He nodded. "Thank you."

We hurriedly got dressed and left the bathroom. I felt lighter than I had in a long time, and I was ready to take on whatever came next.

"All right, Ryker," I said. "What have you got for us?"

"These guys are Taranis worshippers." She played the recording.

"Gabeta en druthan!"

This roughly translates to 'find and grab'," she told us. *"This next part..."*

She fast-forwarded to, *"Naton destutu mi, druidacos se tonaros."*

"Don't fail your god, Tonaros, which is just another name for Taranis. That's what the Gauls, who were pre-Celts, called him. The ones who escaped and the ones the Roman's enslaved took their religion with them, and Tonaros became Taran, Toranos, and more. All his incarnations, he is the god of thunder."

"Like Thor," Veronica said.

Ryker nodded. "He predates Thor. He even predates the Roman god Jupiter. There is speculation, that the god Jupiter was really just Taranis hedging his bets."

"May the best worshipper win," I muttered.

"Exactly," she said. "But it's not anything that can be proven."

The football coach in Southhill Village, Jordan Sonnavilsa, was one of Odin's many half-human children. Odin was Thor's father. "Does that mean Odin is Taranis's father too?"

Ryker pursed her lips as mirth lit her eyes. "No. Thor isn't an incarnation of Taranis. While he got the name the god of thunder, it's only because of his hammer, *Mjolnir*, had the power to harness electricity from the air. The hammer was made as part a of bet, but that's a long story, and one that anyone can look up." She waved her hand. "Needless to say, Thor isn't a god. He just plays one on TV."

Veronica stifled a giggle.

Ryker hit the play button again.

I don't know if he is with the people in the house, but it's ten at night, so I'm guessing he is." Then the loud pounding occurred, once again kicking up my fear for Rowan. *"Gamaros uetonos, Doktoros Everlee, agus non se denkas."*

She stopped. "Come out, Doctor Everlee. I know you're in there."

"That one was pretty straight forward," Carver said. "I thought it was something like, that but it didn't help trying to search the words, even with context. The internet really doesn't have much at all on Gaulish."

"It's a dead language for a reason," Ryker stated. "I only learned it because I had been contracted to hunt down an empousa, which is basically a vampire that seduces and feeds on men."

"Tough job," Veronica said. Then added, "For the vampire, I mean."

Ryker shook her head, but a slight smile tugged at her lips. "It turned out she wasn't an empousa, she was a mormo."

"I know this one," I said. I touched on the women in Greco-Roman mythology in my Women's Studies courses. "Mormo was a woman who ate her own children and after, she got used as the boogeyman to keep all the kids in line."

"That's the myth, but it's not the truth. Mormolyca was a servant woman for a wealthy man. He forced himself on her and forced her to have four of his children, each one presented as slaves for his wife. When Mormalyca tried to escape with the children, she was captured, locked in a room with them, and they were burned alive. Her brutal death created a vengeful spirit that came back an killed all the wealthy man's children, and that's how the mythology began."

My stomach twisted in a knot. "Holy shitballs. That's the most awful thing I've ever heard," Veronica said.

"I wish it was the most awful thing I've heard," Ryker replied. "Anyhow, the mormo I was hired to track down, wasn't actually a mormo. She was the spirit of a Gaul woman whose children and husband were killed during the Gallic wars. She'd been wandering for thousands of years, unable to rest. I took pity on her and made it my mission to figure out how to help her move one without tearing apart her soul."

"And that's how you learned Gaulish," I said.

She grinned. "And that's how I learned Gaulish. It took me about two years to figure out how to help her, so she stayed with me until it was time for her to go." She clicked the play button again.

"*Cumascertos, Mapos Taranou, agus bidis ulamuros. Surrender, and you won't be harmed, Doktoros Everlee. Resist, and you will wish for death.*"

"We make preparations. There will be an accord." She shook her head. "Something like that. Ulam is willing or prepared, and uros means ready."

"Ready and willing," I muttered. "But for what? Iris had faced some nasty druids who'd wanted to sacrifice her for power. I was certain I'd heard the named Taranis during that ordeal." I looked at Carver. "Wasn't that wheel that sucked Evan away a Taranis wheel?"

"Yep," Carver said.

"Could this be revenge for that?" I didn't think gods and goddesses really cared whether their worshippers won or lost. From what I could divine, the gods and goddesses were all about playing the game.

"I don't think so," Ryker said. "Cumascertos loosely translates to an accord or an agreement."

My brows hurt with how hard they were furrowing. "I don't get it?"

"I think these guys were hired," Ryker said.

"By who?"

"*Mapos Taranou*," she replied. "The son of Taranis."

"Well, that doesn't sound good." I pivoted my gaze to Zev. "Do you know a son of Taranis?"

He shook his head. "I've never had any dealings with Taranis, with the exception of helping Iris with her problem. Even then, my involvement was brief."

"If this was about that situation," Carver interjected. "Iris would be the target, not Zev."

Zev nodded. "I agree."

"Is there someone we can call who might know who this son could be?" I asked.

"I'm the one people call." Ryker shoved her hands in her pockets. "But I don't have any information. This is the first I've heard of a son. He's one of the few gods who doesn'thave little demi-gods running around."

"Until now," I added.

She shrugged. "If this person who hired these guys is truly the son of Taranis, then yeah, until now."

"Dayamn," Veronica said. "So what are we going to do?"

I looked at the feisty kitchen witch. "You should go home. You've done so much for us already, and this is going to get extremely dangerous."

"You'll have to fight me off with a stick—a huge one," she said defiantly. "I'm sticking around to see how this turns out. Plus, I know the ins and outs of this town better than any of you."

"She has a point," Carver admitted.

I glanced around the room, taking in the faces—determined, loyal, and maybe just a little reckless. Three things that described me to a tee. But as much as I wanted to believe we had some kind of leg up because we knew the plan, a nagging voice whispered that there was something bigger lurking behind the red velvet curtain.

And if that nagging voice turned out to be right, I'd burn the whole damn curtain down along with the stage and the entire town. I would do whatever it took to keep the people I loved safe.

Chapter Fourteen

CARVER PULLED UP A MAP OF THE AREA AROUND The Grand Treehouse Resort on his phone, zooming in on the dense forest surrounding the cabins. "Trees surround the whole place," he said, "but if these guys have Rowan, they've probably set up perimeter alerts and magical wards. Maybe even cameras or tripwires."

"They also gave us enough time to show up before the deadline," I added, frowning. "That feels... off. Why give us a head start unless they want us to arrive early? It definitely feels like a setup." Was Zev's disappearance and bandishing part of the trap? If it had been, they'd failed. Would they know they'd failed? I guess that fact that he wasn't smoke in a bottle somewhere would give this son of Taranis a clue."

"It reeks of a trap," Carver agreed, his arms crossed. "But not trying isn't an option. Not with Rowan's life on the line."

"Nobody's talking about not trying," I told him. "We just want to be smart about it so we don't put Ro in more danger. Here's what we know. The people who have Rowan want Zev. They gave us two days to deliver him. That's a lot of time, considering I live a short driving distance from Eureka Springs. Veronica saw the top knot dude drive into the Grand Treehouse Resort. We verified that his people are there. Lots of white SUVs, lots of big, dangerous-looking dudes who would happily break our faces."

There was also Kah'ar, Zev's sister. I wasn't as sure of her innocence as Zev, but I knew if we found evidence of her evolvement, I wouldn't have to tell the gang, he would. I glanced at him, and he inclined his head in an affirmative. Good.

"Do we know Rowan's there for certain?" I continued. "Nope. Do we still have to check the place out? Absolutely. But let's keep some perspective here. We can't rush in blind without getting the lay of the land, learning what defenses they have in place, and verifying that Rowan is even there. Acting rash is the very thing that will ensure Rowan's life is on the line.

Carver gave a curt nod. "I know. I'm just..."

I put my hand on his shoulder. "Same. I promise you I want to go in, guns blazing, as badly as you do, but acting rash could get him killed."

"Says the woman who launched herself at a stranger for standing on her sister's porch," Veronica said with an admiring smile.

I had always been impulsive, leaping without looking—even when looking would've saved me a lot of bumps and bruises. I felt that Veronica and I had more in common than I wanted to admit. She reminded me a lot of my younger self, always searching for the next bright and shiny thing. Not that I had changed all that much. I had a strong sense of justice and a hair-trigger temper. The combination could make me volatile, but that was only when my safety was at risk.

I looked at the young witch. "Putting my own life in danger is one thing. I'm not so careless with the lives of other people."

Zev stepped behind me and put his arms around me. "I find your willingness to fight a foe more powerful than yourself both exciting and terrifying."

I leaned my head back onto his shoulder. "Same, love. Same."

I shivered as my body reacted to the sound of his low, sexy chuckle.

"Back to the matter at hand," Carver said. "We

have to figure out a way to get close enough to have eyes on the cabins. Our main priority is figuring out which cabin Rowan is being held in."

I nodded, an idea forming. "If we can find a secluded spot around the edge of the property, I might be able to find a critter, like a raccoon or something, to scout ahead for us."

Veronica snorted. "You can't actually talk to animals. Right?"

Ryker smirked. "Oh, she can. Ask the drug cartel in Mexico we escaped from thanks to a coati named Racón. He led us through a hidden cave system, no questions asked."

"It's true," Carver chimed in, grinning. "She's got a mole at her house that's basically her roommate."

I laughed. "More like a property mate. Tupo's a gentleman. He agrees not to tear up my yard, and I let him bring his lady friends back during mating season."

"Generous arrangement," Veronica said, her voice tinged with incredulity.

I wondered briefly how Tupo, his temporary mate—since moles didn't mate for life—and his new baby were doing. The thought warmed me, even in the middle of the mess we were facing.

Zev shot me a look of admiration. He didn't say anything, but I could feel the pride in his gaze.

"If you really can talk to animals," Veronica said, her tone skeptical but curious, "then I might have an idea."

"Well, don't keep us waiting, witch," Ryker said, leaning forward. "Spit it out."

Veronica took out her phone, unlocked the screen, and pulled up her Pinstagram feed.

Incredibly, the account was titled "Mr. Whispers: Adventures of a Black Cat."

"Mr. Whispers has a social media account?" I asked, making a mental note to follow him when this was all over.

"Yes," she said sheepishly. "I make a few grand every month from advertisers, so don't judge me too harshly. It pays the bills."

"Judging?" Ryker gave her a wide stare. "I plan on subscribing to that cat and feeding the machine."

"What did you want to show us?" Carver asked.

"Here," she said, opening the first video. "I'll just show you."

The clip showed a chaotic view of her apartment, the camera jerking wildly as it moved over tables, under the couch, and through the kitchen. In the background, a raspy meow rang out, unmistakably Mr. Whispers, Veronica's black cat. The video ended with the cat slipping into view of a mirror. The small button camera on his collar gleamed as he flopped onto his back, stretching a paw toward his reflection.

"He's adorable," Ryker said. "But you can't be thinking of sending that cute ball of fluff on a reconnaissance mission."

"Not him," Veronica said excitedly. "But if Marigold can find a squirrel or some other animal willing to wear the camera..."

"That could actually work," I said, my mind spinning with the possibility. "The camera could show us what's inside the cabins without us getting too close."

Carver stroked his chin thoughtfully. "I can't think of any reason not to try it."

"It's settled, then," Veronica said. "I'll go home and grab the camera."

"Do you have any fresh rosemary?" Carver asked her. "I've got an idea for a spell, but it'll take a freshly cut sprig. All I've got in my kit is dried."

Veronica preened. "What kind of kitchen witch would I be without a rosemary bush? The second bedroom in my apartment is a grow room. I might have other things you'll want."

"If you have a grow room, you most definitely will have other stuff I'll want," Ryker said with a grin, miming a joint.

Veronica grinned. "I might have a little of that, too."

"We'll all go," I said firmly. "I want to test my ability to communicate with Mr. Whispers before we head to the resort. Better safe than sorry. But nobody's getting stoned until this is over."

Ryker laughed. "Spoilsport."

"I like her," Veronica said, giving Ryker the once-over.

"Aww," Ryker said, giving Veronica's nose a boop. "Don't be too hasty. Wait until you get to know me."

"Let's get going." Carver closed the screen on his phone and then put it in his pocket. "I'll put a 'Do Not Disturb' sign on the suite door. Don't need housekeeping finding the scorched bed."

"Good idea," I said, feeling guilty about the mess I'd made of his room. Still, getting Zev back had been worth a few thousand dollars in property damage.

We waited until Carver hung the sign on the door, then left the hotel and headed toward Veronica's apartment above the Grotto Coffee Shop. Halfway there, I spotted the white SUV I'd seen circling the hotel earlier. My heart jumped into my throat.

"There," I whispered, pointing. "That's the vehicle I saw when I woke up from my nap."

Everyone ducked into a narrow alley with no exit. It was a tight squeeze, and we held our breath, waiting for the SUV to pass. But it didn't keep going. It stopped directly across the street from us.

"Damn it," Carver muttered.

Zev's voice was calm but firm. "I can get us out of here if it becomes necessary."

"And take us where?" Ryker hissed. "You need a clear landing spot, and transporting all of us could end with someone inside a wall."

"I don't want to be in a wall," Veronica whined.

I swallowed hard, my pulse pounding. "Let's hope it doesn't come to that."

The SUV's engine idled in front of The Clucking Hen restaurant across the street, and I clenched my fists. What were the chances we'd go unnoticed? Don't look over here, don't look over here, were the words I played on repeat in my head. Whatever was coming, I had a sinking feeling we'd just run out of time to plan.

The SUV engine cut, and a sinking feeling hit me square in the gut. We were caught between a rock and a hard place—or, in this case, a blocked-off alley and who knew how many kidnapping brutes. The tinted windows on the vehicle revealed nothing, and I held my breath as the passenger door opened.

In what could only have been seconds but

stretched into what felt like minutes, a tiny old lady emerged, feet first. She clung to the door for support, wobbling slightly as she worked her way out of the SUV. From the driver's side, an older gentleman shuffled around to her. He retrieved a walker from the back seat, unfolding it with slow, deliberate care, before handing it to her.

At what could generously be described as a snail's pace, the couple made their way into the restaurant, the woman gripping the walker with both hands.

For a moment, none of us said anything. Then Ryker broke the silence. "Uh, guys? Unless they plan to beat us with their Medicare cards or poison us with glaucoma meds, I think we're safe."

A burst of laughter erupted from the group, the tension shattering in an instant.

I shrugged, feeling a little silly. "It's not paranoia if people are out to get you," I said, grinning despite myself.

Carver said, "I find your newfound caution endearing."

I smacked his shoulder. "Smart ass."

"Takes one to know one."

Still chuckling, we stepped out of the alley and onto Spring Street. The tension still hummed faintly in the back of my mind. I kept a wary eye out for more white SUVs, and I knew I wasn't the only one.

The restaurant was closed. "I close up at two on weekdays," Veronica explained. "It usually goes dead by one."

"This is a nice place," Ryker told her. "It's yours?"

Veronica shook her head. "It's the landlord's, but I do a fair job of running the place. Plus, it gives me somewhere to live where the rent isn't an arm and a leg."

Ryker ran her hand through her bright purple hair. "I'm glad you get to keep all your limbs. They can come in pretty handy."

"I've been known to be handy," Veronica said.

"Handy or handsy?" I asked.

The kitchen witch laughed. "Either works."

We climbed the stairs to her apartment on the second floor. Seeing the place in full color was a revelation. Where it had looked gothy-light in grayscale, now it was vibrant, with pops of pinks, bright blues, and purples among all the black. It reminded me of one of Michael's manga novels, all bold contrasts, bright colors and eye-catching detail.

She must've noticed my interest because she said, "I'm into kawaii goth. It puts the fun in dysfunctional."

"I can dig it," Ryker said. The half-djinn was a pure punk goddess warrior, with a style that screamed rebellion. There was nothing cutesy about her, yet she managed to look impressed.

"That's a big compliment," I told Veronica.

"Well, thanks," the young witch said, a blush creeping up her cheeks.

Interesting. I hadn't thought anything could make her blush, but there it was.

"Mr. Whispers," Veronica cooed. "We have company."

The sleek black cat padded into the living room with a regal air, his tail high as he gave us a once-over. "It's about time," he said indignantly. "My bed needs fluffing. How do you expect me to sleep in an unfluffed bed? My potty palace needs scooping, and my water bowl is nearly dry. I could've starved or died of thirst, and then you'd have come home to a dried husk of a cat." He swished his tail at the kitchen witch as he wove his body between her legs. "Is that what you want, Veronica? A dried husk of a cat?"

I laughed at the miniature tyrant's tirade.

"What?" Veronica asked, narrowing her eyes at me. "What did he say?"

"All I'm hearing is a bunch of meow-myow-myows," Carver said, shaking his head.

"Same," Ryker added, smirking.

I smiled at Mr. Whispers. He plopped down, raised a paw, and began grooming his toes, looking detached and unaffected by the conversation. His eyes flicked up at me. "Go on, human. Translate my genius."

"You got it, Mr. Whispers." I turned to Veronica and said, "He wants you to know that he's fully aware he hit the owner jackpot and feels very lucky to live here."

The cat flopped onto his back and tilted his head at me. "Close enough, human," he said lazily. "Close enough."

Veronica beamed, scooping him up and cradling him like a baby. She scratched his tummy as she cooed, "Aww, who's my good, sweet boy?"

"I am," Mr. Whispers said with a self-satisfied purr. "Obviously."

I chuckled softly, shaking my head. With my ability to converse with animals confirmed, we could move forward with the plan. Knowing my mojo was back gave me a boost of confidence.

Once Mr. Whispers had been properly spoiled and set down, Veronica fetched his small button camera collar and held it up. "Here it is. Light-weight, durable, and perfect for a squirrel or raccoon."

"Great," I said. "Let's hope I can find a willing volunteer when we get there."

Veronica led Carver into her second bedroom, with Ryker following on their heels. Zev and I stayed in the living room for a moment of peace so I could gather my thoughts. We sat on the couch, and I reclined into his arms, his quiet presence steadying me.

"This is going to work," I said, breaking the silence first.

"Damn straight." I thought about my family, how we were raised to be independent and self-reliant, and how we learned to lean on and trust the people we loved and who loved us. "I'm an Everlee. Everlee's know how to win."

He rubbed my arms. "They certainly do."

By the time Veronica, Carver, and Ryker returned with a basket of fresh herbs, we were ready to leave.

"Let's do this," I said, standing up.

All we had to do was convince a forest critter to do some double-oh-seven spy work, find any wards or traps that needed undoing, get inside the resort undetected, and free my brother without gigantic, terrifying Gallic muscle-heads killing any of us.

Easy peasy, right?

We'd have to wait and see...

Chapter Fifteen

THERE WAS AN APARTMENT COMPLEX AT THE edge of town, half a mile from the resort if we went through the woods. Veronica had a friend who lived there, so she was confident that leaving her car wouldn't attract any attention. I sat between Carver and Zev in the backseat. Carver had been filling cloth drawstring bags, the kind that I'd used in the past when making sachets for my linen drawers. He'd stuffed them with herbs, including fresh rosemary, crushed obsidian, hematite, and clear quartz for amplification, with several drops each of lavender and cedarwood oils.

My eyes were watering and my nose was dripping as the mix of acrid, pungent, woodsy, and floral aromas choked the air. Veronica's car reeked.

It was the only moment I wished my nose was still broken.

"Damn, Carver," Ryker complained with a small gag. "You couldn't have put those together before we got in the car?"

He began passing the bags around, giving one to each of us. "No pain. No gain. These are protection bags. They should be able to deflect simple hexes and curses, and if you get in trouble, they can amplify other spells."

"I don't have other spells," Ryker said.

"I do," Carver said. He began distributing small ampules with colored bands at the neck. There was enough for two each. "The red are distractions—minor explosions, stink bombs, flash-bang, that sort of thing. The blue are shield spells. Once we find Ro, we can use them to put up barriers. It'll keep the bad guys at bay for about thirty seconds, give or take. Hopefully, enough time to get the hell away."

I held up a yellow-banded vial. "And these?"

"Careful with those. Don't get any on you." He held up one of them, and the swirling mixture inside was iridescent. "It's a paralysis potion. It will freeze someone in place."

"That's a cool trick," Veronica said. "For how long?"

"Again, about thirty seconds," Carver said.

"Hopefully, long enough for Zev to apparate Rowan to safety while we escape."

Zev raised a brow.

"There's no telling what condition he'll be in when we find him." Carver's voice was strained. "He'll be the most vulnerable out of all of us."

I met Zev's pensive gaze and nodded. "That's what I want, too." Zev was the actual target. He wouldn't be around for the bad guys to snatch if he were busy rescuing my brother.

His expression remained contemplative before he looked away briefly and gave me a slight nod. "If that's what you wish."

"It is," I told him, not trusting his agreement. I might not be able to hear his thoughts, but I could feel the rising conflict inside him. He was spoiling for a fight and didn't want to be left out.

"That's not what I'm feeling." His tone was gentle. "I don't know if I can leave you behind," he admitted. "But I will try."

"Oh, Zev." I pressed my palm to his cheek and felt our bond flare through the mark. "I promise my survival instincts will be at an all-time high."

"Unless someone you care about is in danger."

He wasn't wrong. "My survival instincts will be at an all-time high... unless someone I care about is in danger, and then it will be high enough for the both of us. I promise."

"As you say, my love." He opened the door and got out of the car. He gestured toward the apartment complex. "I need to find a safe area to transport your brother when the time comes."

I got out of the car after him. "It's a big parking lot."

He gestured to a car driving out. "And anyone can park in it. I wouldn't want to plant him in the motor of a minivan. I'll find a place that won't be used."

I was horrified by the idea of Rowan fused to a vehicle. "Good idea." I nodded, then looked at the woods, thick with trees, just past the parking lot. "I'm going to see if I can find a critter who's willing to play ball."

"Or, in this case, Candid Camera," Ryker said.

"What's that?" Veronica asked, suddenly making me feel very old.

"You've never heard of *Candid Camera?* The show where they secretly film people getting pranked."

She frowned. "You mean *Punk'd?*"

"Nope, I sure don't." I waved a hand. "But you know what, it's fine. If you watched *Punk'd*, you kind of get the gist." Only *Candid Camera* was way funnier.

Veronica handed me the collar with the camera. She had her phone in her other hand. "I've got the live feed ready to go. I'll turn it on at your signal."

"Great," I told her, taking the collar cam.

"Good luck," she said. "It took me two weeks of easing Mr. Whispers into wearing it without trying to rip his own head off."

I arched a brow at her. "Thanks for the pep talk."

She winced and tried to hide a smile. "Sorry."

I crossed the grass into the tree line. The woods were quiet, except for the occasional rustle of leaves. The faint hum of activity in the distance—the buzz of insects, the wind catching the tops of the trees— reminded me how close we were to the cabins. The place where danger waited. Thankfully, I didn't sense a magical ward. If they'd placed one, it was closer to the cabins. It didn't take long to hear the telltale rustling of branches or the high-pitched alarms chirping and excited chattering of squirrels on alert. What they said was the equivalent of an '80s after-school special warning children about stranger danger. Unfortunately, most of the danger to children was from people they knew, so stranger-danger campaigns did little to keep kids safe.

"Hey," I said, volume loud enough for them to

hear me but not so loud as to attract people's attention to the maxi-skirted woman in the middle of the woods. One of the squirrels, a pretty good-sized fella, stopped yapping and started flicking his tail as if to tell his army of nut eaters to fall back. "Yeah, you," I told him. "I'm talking to you."

He said, "Wild human. Intruder. Hide."

"Hide from what?" I asked him.

"Intruder," he screamed. "Warning, it speaks! It understands. No come out. Stay hidden!"

Two smaller squirrels jumped from one limb to another, one shoving the other out of the way so they could be the first to see the lady who speaks their language.

"Ovi, Doub!" the larger squirrel shouted. "Back."

"Hi, Ovi." I waved to the younger squirrels. "Doub." I pointed to myself. "I'm Marigold."

"Mar-ee-gold," one of them squealed with delight. "Mar-ee-gold," the other repeated. I had a feeling Ovi and Doub were from the same litter. Their playful, curious nature marked them at four or five weeks old. Ah, the folly of youth. They hadn't learned to be afraid yet.

"Stop. No talk," the larger squirrel demanded. "What you want? Why come my territory?"

His territory, huh? I had read that female squirrels were in charge. They picked what males they wanted to mate with and might pick a dozen during their one-day mating window. The males didn't even have anything to do with raising the babies, which made me think this chonky chatterbug might be female.

"What's your name?" I asked the squirrel.

"Biv," it said.

Well, that wasn't helpful. "Uhm, are you Ovi and Doub's mother?"

The tail swished in a circle and then shook like a rattle. "Yes," Biv said, giving me a wary stank-eye. "No harm my babies."

Okay, that mystery was cleared up.

"I have no intention of harming you or your babies. I come in peace." I sounded like the guy who gets killed first in a fifties alien movie. I shoved the collar into my skirt pocket and showed my open empty hands. "I'm looking for a squirrel who might be willing to help me. I need to know what's going on in the cabins in that direction." I pointed west toward the Grand Treehouse Resort. "It would just be a quick look around kind of job." My voice went up an octave. "You'd wear a collar with a camera..." Now that I was saying it out loud, the plan sounded more outlandish. What in the world made me think I could turn a squirrel into a spy? "Sorry," I told her. "I'll let you get back to your day." I winced under her withering stare. "Do you know of any raccoons around here who might work for food?"

"Help her, help her," Ovi and Doub chanted.

Their mother flicked her tail and screamed at them. They both jumped to a higher branch.

"Why go there?" Biv demanded. "Bad intruders live there. Danger. Tell boys, no go there."

"Have you been over there already?" I asked her.

"Yes. Bad. No human."

"They're not human?"

Her tiny ears worked back and forth as if she were trying to get a radio signal with an antenna. "Not human. Bad."

Her vocabulary was limited, so I went with another angle. "Was there a human with the bad not humans?"

"Human, human," the boys said with glee.

"So there is?" I made it a question.

Biv reluctantly answered. "One has human head."

I had no idea what that meant, but okay, a human with a head. I'd take that as a good sign. The alternative was unacceptable. "The human, he's my family. Like Ovi and Doub are your family. I'm trying to save him from the bad not humans."

Biv's jaws worked like she was chewing on something, but I hadn't seen her put anything in her mouth. Finally, she said, "I go. I look for you."

"Great!" I said, a little too excited. Ovi and Doub were practically doing somersaults.

"For food," she said slyly. "You make raccoon bargain. I want same."

I put my hand over my mouth to cover the spreading grin. "You got it." She must have misunderstood when I asked if they knew a raccoon who would work for food. Her misunderstanding was my good luck. "What food and how much?" A hard object hit me in the side of the head. I turned sharply to where it came from. Doub and Ovi were doubled over laughing. I looked down at what hit me. It was a pecan nut in the shell.

Biv looked at me. "Those," she said. "Many. Pix of them."

I could buy pecans from any grocery store, but would I have to buy out their entire supply or would a few bags do? "And how much is that?"

She quickly climbed down a tree and scampered to a fallen log. There was a hole in the side. "Fill," she said. "A pix."

It was a small log, not more than eight inches wide. The hole looked to hold a couple of pounds of nuts. "Shelled or unshelled?"

Her little eyes widened. "No understand."

I picked up the nut the boys threw at me and tapped the outside. "Do you want the shells on or off? Just the meat."

"On," she said. Both the boys grumbled. "Last longer."

"Makes sense," I commended her. "You're a good mama."

Her tail fluffed out as if she'd put on her Sunday best. "Tell me, Mar-ee-gold. What want me to do?"

"Well..." I pulled the collar out of my pocket and showed her. "The job starts by putting this on."

She looked appalled but didn't run away. Luckily, it hadn't taken Biv a week to convince, and in less than ten minutes, I'd explained what I needed from her, and that afterward, I'd meet her back here to remove the collar. The bushy squirrel preened as her boys scampered around her, treating her like a hero.

I looked at Ovi and Doub. "I'm going to be just past the trees that way." I pointed toward the parking lot of the apartment complex. "You stay here. When your mom returns, I want you to let me know. I will give you extra nuts if you do a good job."

They both nodded enthusiastically as they agreed. Biv gave me a grateful look. "I've got nephews," I told her after the boys were out of earshot. "I know the moment you tell them not to do something is the very second they decide they're going to."

"Wise Mar-ee-gold." She looked wild with Mr. Whispers' collar around her neck. I had to tighten it to keep it from sliding off her head. "Be well."

"Be well," I said back. "Don't do anything dangerous. If you think the not humans see you, run away."

"Still give food?" she asked.

I smiled. "Still give food."

Biv rubbed her small body against my leg and I gently touched her soft furry head. With a last warning to her boys to obey, she took off. I stood there for a moment, watching Biv vanish into the treetops, her movements quick and purposeful. Her sons, Ovi and Doub, perched on a branch nearby, were already chattering excitedly about the nuts they would earn.

"She'll be fine," I told them, mostly to reassure myself.

I exhaled and made my way back to the parking lot, the crunch of leaves under my feet a soft, steady rhythm. As I emerged from the trees, Zev was standing there, arms crossed, his gaze locked on me like he'd been tracking every sound I made.

"How'd it go?" he asked.

"We've got eyes on the target," I said, brushing dirt from my skirt.

Zev tilted his head. "A squirrel?"

"A very determined squirrel," I told him. "She's a shrewd bargainer as well. We're going to owe her about four pounds of pecans in the shell when the job is done."

He didn't respond, but the faint quirk of his lips suggested he was amused despite himself.

Ryker leaned against the car, arms folded, a bemused smirk on her face. "I never thought I'd be on a hunt with a squirrel as the lead scout."

"I got it!" Veronica said. "Feed's up and running." She tucked her chin in surprise as she held her phone up. "And jumping, and climbing, and woah! She leapt like fifteen feet."

"Oh." I snapped to get their attention before they crowded around Veronica's phone. "Biv, uhm, that's the squirrel's name. Biv said the men at the cabins aren't human."

"I didn't expect they would be," Ryker said. "Did she know what they were?"

I shook my head. "She was just emphatic that they weren't human. Can you read magic over a video feed?"

Ryker pursed her lips, then rubbed the back of her neck. "I'm afraid not."

"I didn't think so." I glanced to Zev. "Can you read auras on a video?"

He shrugged. "I've never tried. Because it's a live recording, I will see what I can see."

I walked over to Carver, who was adjusting the straps on his pack, his expression grim.

"Biv said there was one human." I put my hand on his shoulder.

"Alive?"

I forced a smile I didn't feel. "According to her, he still had his head."

He nodded. His face was a myriad of emotions. "Good. A head is good."

"That's what I said." I patted his back. "Let's go see what those assholes are doing over at the cabins."

As we joined the others, I glanced back at the woods, a chill crawling up my spine despite the warmth of the evening. Somewhere in the danger zone, my brother was waiting. Something not human was keeping him prisoner.

And if we didn't act soon, he'd be out of time.

Chapter Sixteen

THE VIDEO FEED WAS SURPRISINGLY CLEAR, WITH only the occasional buffering. Biv, the squirrel, moved like a pro, leaping onto the roof of the first cabin and darting quickly from window to window. She chirped as she went, but weirdly, through the recording, I couldn't understand her anymore.

A few cars passed by us in the parking lot, their drivers glancing curiously at our group huddled around Veronica's phone before moving on.

"Click Clock video," Veronica had said as an explanation to one curious tenant.

He looked annoyed but the answer satisfied him enough to move on. The soft hum of cicadas buzzed in the background, blending with the occasional crunch of gravel underfoot as someone shifted their weight.

The first cabin's layout was straightforward but charming, with an open and romantic vibe. A fireplace sat near the bed, and beyond it, I spotted a small kitchenette and a snug living room with plush furniture sized to match the cabin's scale. The bathroom wasn't visible, but I figured it was tucked out of sight.

"I don't see anyone," Veronica said, her tone flat as she squinted at the screen.

"That squirrel is fast," Ryker added, shading her eyes from the late afternoon sun as she watched the video.

Biv climbed back onto the roof, then sprang onto a cable strung between the first and second cabins. With the precision of a circus performer, she crossed the distance effortlessly.

"Damn, girl, that was smooth," I said, impressed by the squirrel's light-footed balance.

"Like butter," Veronica agreed.

The second cabin had a slightly different layout but kept the same open studio vibe. There was a fireplace, a spa tub, and a kitchenette leading into a small living room. Two hulking men sat at a tiny dinette table, playing cards. Their broad shoulders and bulky frames filled the space, making the furniture seem even smaller.

"Zev, can you read their auras?" I asked, glancing toward him.

He shook his head, the movement curt. "Magic and modern tech don't mix well."

Their muffled voices drifted faintly through the glass, too quiet to make out. Biv didn't linger. She chattered as she leapt to the next cabin, her movements swift and practiced.

The third cabin had a separate bedroom, and we all gasped when the camera revealed my redheaded brother tied up on the bed. His hands and feet were bound, and they'd blindfolded and gagged him.

"He's alone," I whispered, my throat tightening.

"He looks okay," Carver said softly, his voice catching. "Doesn't he?"

I couldn't see any bruises or blood. True to his word, the gruff kidnapper had kept Rowan unharmed...so far. I silently thanked my brother for playing it smart.

"I'll get him now," Zev said, his voice low but firm. "There's no one there. I can be in and out in seconds."

I reached out and grabbed his arm just as Biv started climbing again. The camera captured the ceiling, and my pulse quickened.

"There!" Ryker said, her voice sharp as she pointed at the screen. "It's a sigil, like the one on the bandish hex." She patted Veronica's arm, her movements quick and urgent. "I saw runes too. Go back."

"I can't," Veronica said, her expression pinched with frustration. "It's a live feed. Once it's over, it'll save as a recording, but I can't rewind right now without disrupting the connection."

I turned to Zev, holding his gaze. The late afternoon sun glinted off his dark hair, casting sharp shadows across his face, making it look even more chiseled than usual.

"That's another bandish trap," I told him, my tone steady but firm. "If you pop in there, you're not popping back out. You'll be smoke, and we'll still be stuck figuring out how to get Rowan. Plus, we'll have to rescue you too."

"I'll go," Carver said, his jaw tightening.

"Don't be stupid," Ryker snapped at him, her hands planted on her hips. "You're not built for stealth."

Carver flexed his fingers, his gaze unwavering. "But Dan is. I picked this body for a reason."

Dan? I'd always assumed Carver had chosen the buff redhead look because it reminded him of Rowan. Apparently, there was more to the transformation than sentiment.

"Zev can boost me to the window," Carver continued, his voice calm but determined. "I'll grab

Rowan. We'll climb out, and Zev can poof us back here. He won't trigger the bandish hex, and we'll have accomplished what we came for."

Zev nodded once, his expression unreadable. "I will do what I can."

I didn't like the plan, not one bit. "I should go," I said, stepping closer to Carver. "He's my brother."

Carver flinched, my words had hit a nerve, but his resolve didn't waver. "That doesn't mean I don't care about him just as much," he said, his voice quieter now. "I want Rowan home more than anything."

The raw honesty in his tone caught me off guard. Rowan might not have been ready to commit to Carver, but Carver was already all in.

"Besides," Carver added, his shoulders squaring. "I'm strong enough to carry him out if he can't walk."

I hesitated, glancing at the woods behind us. The breeze rustled the leaves, the sound almost taunting. My forest giant DNA made me strong—probably stronger than Carver's borrowed body—but I knew this wasn't a fight I'd win.

I turned to Ryker, our resident monster hunter. "What do you think?"

Ryker crossed her arms, her expression thoughtful as she looked between us. Another car slowed as it passed, the driver giving us a curious glance before continuing down the lot. The tension in the air thickened, like the heat shimmering off the asphalt.

"Guys," Veronica said, snapping us out of it. "Biv is at the fifth cabin, and I think you better come see this. It's top-knot dude, and he's fighting with some woman."

A woman? That threw me. I hadn't expected a woman to be part of a group of Taranis worshippers. He was kind of a man's god—brutal and aggressive.

"Hurry," Veronica urged. "Biv's on the move."

We crowded around the phone as Biv scurried up the side of the cabin and perched by the window. The screen showed the woman's side profile for just a moment before Biv shifted position. I squinted, trying to catch more details, but the angle changed again as the squirrel climbed to a different window.

Then I saw him. Top-knot guy. His bronze skin gleamed under the cabin's soft lighting, and his pearly hair caught the glow like molten silver. His massive arms were rigid at his sides as the woman— who had her back to the camera—jabbed a finger into his chest. She was shouting, her movements brusque and angry, but her words didn't carry through the glass.

"She's really pissed," I said, keeping my voice low.

"So is he," Ryker added, leaning in closer.

Biv shifted again, giving us a clearer view of the man's face. His features were striking—his jaw strong and angular, his nose sharp but elegant, and his mouth full and set in a hard line. "Enough!" he bellowed loud enough we could hear him through the video feed. Then, his calm completely eroded, his hands erupted in flames that blazed up his arms as tendrils of fire licked from his eyes.

"Oh my God," I thought, but Ryker and Carver beat me to the punchline.

"Ifrit," they said in unison.

My stomach twisted. My hands felt clammy as I turned to Zev. "Why? Why would an ifrit come after you?"

Zev's expression darkened, his jaw tightening as he stared at the screen. "I don't know," he said. "I don't recognize him.'

On the screen, the woman turned, giving us our first real look at her face. Her cheeks were flushed with rage, her eyes narrowed and blazing, but I saw something else too...fear. Then, in a flash, she snapped her fingers and vanished into thin air.

"Uh, what was that?" Veronica asked, her tone both bewildered and uneasy.

I glanced at Zev, hoping for an answer.

His face had gone pale, his usual calm had been

replaced with something akin to dread. "That," he said quietly, "was Kah'ar. My sister."

"Sister?" Ryker asked. "You have a sister?"

I have many sisters," Zev told her. "Kah'ar is one of my eldest siblings. She's four hundred years older than me."

That was new information for me, but I'd only found out he had a sister earlier in the day. She'd been the person he'd been trying to contact to translate the Gaulish on the dictation recorder. The one he'd been texting when he disappeared for two hours this morning. Damn it. I'd worried she was a part of this. He'd betrayed her by helping the Romans, and after over two thousand years, she was finally getting her revenge.

"No." Zev's tone was firm. "I don't believe Kah'ar would do this."

"You said you hadn't seen her for over one hundred years. When was the last time you'd seen her before then? She was heartbroken. You know how you would feel if you thought your sister was responsible for my death."

"I do," he agreed, "but she wouldn't seal me away with a bandish. For a djinn, that's the closest we can get to death. Reduced to smoke for an eternity, at the mercy of those who find us and use us for their greed, lust, and power." He shook his head, the denial written across his face. "She told me she understood. She hadn't forgiven me, but it was a start..." His voice faded, heavy with emotion.

"I understand why you want to believe her," I said, taking his hands in mine. "She's your sister. You care about her. But her image wasn't conjured out of thin air. She's here with the ifrit, and she's a part of this, one way or another."

Zev closed his eyes, his face pinching with pain. When he opened them, his irises burned with molten fire. "I don't know if I can stop her," he said, his voice raw.

"Because you can't, or because you won't?" I pressed.

His silence was the only answer I got. I understood more than most. If Iris—or any of my sisters—turned bad, I didn't know if I'd be able to stop them either. But I'd want someone else to do it for me. I squeezed his hands. "I will," I promised. "If I can, I'll stop her for you."

He nodded slowly, his expression bleak. "When the time comes, I'll show you the way."

The others had been quiet during our exchange, the tension palpable. Finally, Veronica broke the silence. "Am I missing something here?" she asked, raising an eyebrow.

"My sister," Zev said without hesitation, his

voice steady now, "was the person I contacted to translate the Gaulish. She was in love with a Gallic warrior, and I used her connection with him to give Caesar the information he needed to win the war and conquer Gaul."

"Holy shit," Veronica blurted. Her eyes widened, and then she waved her hand in dismissal. "Wait, sorry, sorry. Not important. You knew Caesar?"

Ryker spoke next, her tone sharp as she ignored Veronica's outburst and looked straight at me. "You should've told us," she said.

My brow furrowed at her accusation. "It wasn't my story to tell."

"But it was information we needed to know," she shot back.

Her indignation set my teeth on edge. "Was it? And what would you have done with it?" I challenged.

Ryker opened her mouth but faltered. "I would have..." Her words trailed off.

"Exactly," I said, cutting her off. "You would've done exactly what we're doing now—recon, then rescue. Nothing has changed. We came here for information, and now we have it." I softened my tone. "Are we good?"

Ryker frowned, still irritated, but, after a moment, she nodded curtly. "We're good."

"Great." I turned to address the group. "Now we know there are two ifrits involved in this. That's bad, but at least we're not going in blind." A thought clicked into place. "That bandish hex—does it work on all djinns, or is it tied to a specific one? Like Zev?"

Ryker chewed her bottom lip, thinking it over. "It's possible."

"So," I said slowly, "if that ifrit or Kah'ar were to walk under that bandish sigil in the room with Rowan, might be trapped?"

Ryker's eyes lit up with realization. "You want to trap the djinn in their own trap? Cool. But how do we get them there?"

I sighed. "No, that's not what I meant, but if we can do that, I wouldn't be opposed."

"Then what are you thinking?" she asked.

"That the djinn can't enter Rowan's room," Carver said. "That's probably why the muscle is here. Someone has to keep him in the room. If we can get inside, we can get him out fast. If worst comes to worst, we only have to deal with the bodyguards."

"I like your optimism," I said, giving him a tight smile. "But those bodyguards aren't human, and we don't know what they are. Fighting them might not be as easy as a one-two punch."

Carver's eyes softened, pleading. "We have to try."

"Hey, Avengers," Veronica interrupted, holding up her phone. "Biv is heading back to the woods."

"That could work to our advantage," I said, snapping into focus. "Biv can keep watch while we sneak in from the back to get Rowan. You can monitor the feed. If anyone comes, I'll have her drop down, and that'll be our signal that the shit is hitting the fan."

"And if it hits the fan?" Veronica asked nervously.

"Create a distraction," Ryker said.

Veronica blinked, her wide eyes searching for answers. "How?"

Ryker tapped her chin. "You're creative. I'm sure you'll think of something."

Veronica groaned but didn't argue.

"So we're doing this?" Carver asked, his gaze bouncing between us.

"I think so." I turned to Zev for confirmation.

He inclined his head. "Yes."

"Ryker, you and Zev stick together. We shouldn't chance your djinn lineage rearing its ugly head. We can't lose you to the hex. Besides, you and Zev have the best chance kicking those Gaul freaks' asses if it comes down to a fight.

"Good plan," Ryker approved. "Do we wait for dark?"

I shook my head. "Daytime gives us the element of surprise. They won't expect us to try a rescue while it's still light out, and the cabin backs up to the woods. The pine trees will give us plenty of cover."

Ryker scratched the shaved side of her head, a slow grin spreading across her face. "A daytime sneak attack. I like it."

I wasn't sure I did, but what choice did we have? We were either getting Rowan out of there, or we were about to step into a shit storm—most likely both. At least we were going in with our eyes wide open.

Chapter Seventeen

THE WIND RUSTLED THROUGH THE TREES, THE pine scent mingling with the faint tang of adrenaline. I crouched by the tree line, Biv perched on my shoulder, chittering softly as if to reassure herself she was getting paid double the nuts for this nonsense.

"This has to work," Carver whispered, his voice low. He adjusted his grip on the trunk of the massive pine we were about to climb. The back window of Cabin No. 3 glinted faintly in the late afternoon sun, golden beams piercing through the trees.

I glanced at him, then back at Biv. "It will. She's keeping watch. Aren't you, Biv?" I rubbed her tiny head, and she flicked her tail in what I hoped was a confident nod.

Biv chirped. "Double nuts. No tricks."

"No tricks," I promised. "Now go, keep an eye on

those brutes. Just drop down if it gets dangerous, and then go and hide."

"Watch. Drop. Hide," she repeated as she leapt from my shoulder, her bushy tail a streak of gray as she darted back into the branches.

I turned to Carver. "Quick and easy, down and dirty. I'll set the wards on the door to the living room while you untie Rowan. We'll lay a few of those offensive spells you made as a backup, then get the hell out the same way we came in."

Carver nodded. "Got it." He tapped his earbud. "Veronica, we're moving in."

Veronica's voice crackled through. "Copy that. I'm watching the feed. No movement around the cabins right now."

I took a deep breath, hiked my skirt up, placed my hands on the rough bark, and started climbing. Anyone who tells you that climbing a pine is fun, has never had a sharp stick in the eye. The sticky, pokey branches were for the birds. Carver followed behind me, his broader frame making the climb slower but steady. As I pulled myself onto a sturdy branch near the back window of the treehouse, I glanced toward the woods where Zev and Ryker were watching. Ryker gave me a thumbs-up from her perch in a nearby tree. Zev remained still, his fiery eyes scanning the area below.

The window was slightly ajar. So far, so good. I carefully pushed it open, wincing at the faint creak.

"Shit," I heard Carver hiss. "I dropped the phone."

"Can you reach it?"

"No," he said. "It fell down through the branches. I can't see it."

Ah hell. The pit in my stomach widened. We were going in blind. "Come on," I told him. "We're here. Let's just get this done."

Carver sighed. "No more Veronica."

I nodded and slipped inside, my boots landing softly on the wooden floor. Rowan was on the bed, half on his side, his hands tied behind him and his legs bound at the ankles. His head turned toward the faint sound of me entering, but the blindfold kept him from seeing me.

I moved quickly, pulling out the vials Carver had prepared earlier. I smashed the first blue vial at the base of the door, watching the shimmering shield rise to cover the entrance. The smell of cedar and lavender filled the room, masking the stale air. Another red vial went at the window, creating a barrier to keep any unwelcome guests from sneaking in behind us.

"Get him free," I whispered to Carver as he

made his way to Rowan, crouching by the bed. I went to set the barrier spell on the door.

"Hey, Ro," Carver whispered, his voice soft as he started working on the knots. "It's me. It's going to be okay."

Rowan didn't respond, but he held unnaturally still as Carver untied his wrists and ankles, then gently removed the blindfold and gag. His wide eyes darted around then landed on Carver, confusion clouding his expression.

"It's okay," Carver said again, his voice soothing. "We're here to get you out."

Rowan sat up, staring at Carver for a moment. To my utter shock, he rolled from the bed, grabbed a wooden chair near the bed, and moving faster than I had expected from my brother, he swung the chair and smashed it into the side of Carver's head.

Carver crumpled to the floor. Rowan straddled him, ready to hit him again.

"Ro, stop!" I shouted, rushing forward and grabbing his arm. "It's Carver! He's under a transformation spell!"

Rowan froze, blinking at me in shock. "Mare?" I'd thought he'd seen me but he acted like my face had just registered to him.

"Yes, it's me," I said firmly. "And that's Carver. You just knocked him out."

Rowan's face paled as he turned Carver onto his back. He looked down at the strange redhead he'd smacked to the floor and stared incredulously.

"Yes," I confirmed. "I know it doesn't look like him, but that's Carver."

"Carver?" His voice cracked. "Oh, shit. Oh no. I'm sorry," His hands trembled as he cradled Carver's face. "Carver, I'm sorry. I thought...I don't know what I thought. It's been a really crappy few days. Wake up. Please, wake up."

I watched, stunned, as Rowan leaned down and desperately kissed Carver's lips. As if right out of a fairytale, Carver's eyes fluttered open, and the illusion faded. His buff, redheaded form shimmered and melted away, leaving his usual lanky frame, disheveled dark hair, and piercing blue eyes.

Carver smiled weakly at my brother. "Did you just kiss me in front of your sister?"

Rowan froze, glancing up at me with wide, surprised eyes. "I—uh—"

"Hey, love is love, man," I said with a shrug, though I couldn't help the small smirk tugging at my lips. "But right now, we need to get the hell out of here."

A loud bang echoed through the room, and I spun toward the door. The brutish kidnappers were pounding against the wards. Carver had said they would only be good for a short time, and it was already starting to falter.

"We're out of time," I said, my voice tight. "Carver, can you stand?"

Rowan didn't wait for an answer. He grabbed Carver's arm and hauled him to his feet, his hands lingering on him as though afraid to let go. "I'm so sorry I hit you," Rowan whispered.

"It's okay," Carver said, wincing as he steadied himself. "I'll be fine."

I hurried to the window and pulled back the curtain, only to see two more of the brutes patrolling outside. Their massive forms cast long shadows in the fading light. My stomach twisted. "We're trapped," I said, spinning back toward the boys. "Any bright ideas?"

Rowan opened his mouth, but Carver cut him off. "We'll follow your lead."

"Hah, thanks." As the next strike shattered the barrier completely, and a horn smashed through the splintered wood. I stumbled back, staring at the sharp point jutting into the room. "What the actual—?"

"What the hell is that?" Rowan asked, his wide eyes darting between me and the door.

Ryker's voice rang out from outside, sharp and

clear through the back window. "They're minotaurs!"

Minotaurs? I stared at the horn, trying to wrap my head around it. "You mean, like, *real* minotaurs? Man body, bull head?" Well crap. Welcome to mythology 101.

The sound of fireballs exploding outside made my pulse race. I didn't know what the hell was happening out there, but we didn't have time to figure it out. The horn wrenched back, and the door groaned under another blow.

"We need a plan," Rowan said, his voice tight. "Something better than wait-and-die."

"Working on it." I scrambled my brain for a solution. Then it hit me—a memory of sitting on the couch with Rose's kids, watching *Percy Jackson and the Lightning Thief*. How did Percy defeat the minotaur again? Oh, yeah. "I've got it!" I said, rushing toward the shattered door. The horn shoved through again, and I grabbed it with both hands.

"What are you doing?" Rowan shouted, staring at me like I'd lost my damn mind.

"I'm trying to rip his freaking horn off! What does it look like? Now get over here and help me!" I barked.

Rowan hesitated for only a second before moving to my side. Carver stepped up too. The three of us grabbed hold of the massive horn, its rough texture biting into our palms.

"On three!" I said. "One, two—pull!"

With a combined Herculean effort, we yanked the horn free. The sound it made was wet and awful, and the creature on the other side of the door let out a deafening bellow of pain and rage. Blood sprayed through the jagged cracks, and the door shuddered as the monster stumbled back.

"What now?" Rowan asked, panting.

I grinned, hefting the horn like a weapon. "Now, we get stabby."

Without waiting for a reply, I reached into my skirt pocket and retrieved the paralyzing potion Carver had given me. My fingers trembled as I uncorked the vial, the iridescent liquid swirling ominously inside. I glanced at Rowan and Carver. "Stay behind me. I've got this."

"Marigold, wait!" Carver started, but I was already moving.

I flung the door open and came face-to-face with the man who had threatened me earlier that day. I recognized his arms, his hair, and his eyes, only now, he didn't look like a human man anymore. His face was twisted, his cow-like nose flaring with each breath. His large ears drooped under the weight of multiple silver rings, and his remaining horn gleamed wickedly in the dim light. His burning eyes locked onto me, filled with pure rage.

"Not today," I said, my voice steady despite the hammering of my heart.

I threw the paralyzing potion at him, and it splashed against his chest. The liquid spread like wildfire, freezing him mid-step. His furious expression remained locked in place as the spell took hold.

I didn't hesitate. Hesitating got you dead. Gripping the massive horn in both hands, I charged forward and drove it into his body. The sharp tip pierced between his ribs, and I gave it a hard push, thrusting upward into where I hoped housed his heart. The impact jolted through my arms, but I didn't stop until the horn was buried.

His wide eyes met mine, and his body trembled as blood bubbled from his lips. He gasped out something in Gaulish, but I didn't need to understand the words to grasp their meaning.

"What did he say?" Rowan asked, his voice tight.

I stepped back as the light drained from the minotaur's eyes. "Something about his god forsaking him," I told my brother as the massive body crumpled to the floor.

I turned back to Rowan and Carver. "Well, that's one down."

Before either could reply, another minotaur was

coming through the front door. "Let's go!" I darted to the back window and peered out, my heart sinking at the sight of two more horned assholes patrolling below.

"We're trapped," I said, spinning back toward the others. "I'm out of ideas."

Rowan opened his mouth to reply, but a ferocious roar from outside cut him off. The sound made my blood run cold. It was Zev.

Then the cabin shook as if it had been rammed by a car, and the minotaur coming through the door was thrown back out. I bolted to the splintered front door to get a look at what hit the cabin. Down below, a white SUV had plowed into one of the support posts of the cabin. The door opened, and Veronica staggered out.

What the hell? She looked up at me, her expression a little dazed, then yelled over the noise of battle, "Come on!"

Smart little witch. She'd gotten creative with a distraction and saved our butts in the process. I turned back to Carver and Rowan. "Get him out of here," I told Carver. "Go, go, go."

Zev stood in the clearing, his flames blazing hotter and brighter than I'd ever seen. Across from him, the ifrit with the top knot hurled fireballs, the air between them shimmering from the inferno. Zev dodged the artillery with supernatural speed, retaliating with a blast of white-hot fire that forced the other ifrit to stagger back.

For a moment, I thought Zev had him.

Then, two of the massive minotaurs charged out of the woods, their horns lowered. They barreled into Zev, grabbing his arms and locking him in place. Zev howled with fury, his entire body erupting into a blazing firestorm. The minotaurs screamed, their flesh sizzling and blackening, but they didn't let go. Even as they burned alive, they held him firm, their sacrifice clearing a path for the "son of Taranis."

The ifrit with the top knot stalked forward, holding a strange metal plate in his hand. My stomach sank as I saw the sigil on the side facing away from him. That had to be another bandish hex. Ryker had said, all it took was a touch.

"Zev, no!" I screamed, my voice cracking with panic. This guy was trying to smoke my djinn, and I wasn't having it. The fire inside me ignited, spreading through my veins like wildfire. Without thinking, I launched myself at the ifrit, flames erupting from my body as I collided with him.

The impact sent us both tumbling to the ground. The metal plate skidded away, landing several feet from us. The ifrit grunted, startled, and scrambled to his feet. He glared at me, flames licking around his body. "You dare challenge me?" he snarled, his voice echoing through the clearing.

"Yeah, I do, assface," I shot back, planting my feet and letting my fire blaze hotter.

He raised his arms to the sky. "Taranis, god of thunder, strike down my enemies and grant me vengeance!"

Lightning crackled in the clouds above. His body surged with power, his flames growing brighter and hotter. He struck me hard in the chest, the force sending me flying across the road. I hit the ground with a painful thud, the breath knocked out of me.

"Marigold!" Zev bellowed through the chaos. His flames erupted like a nuclear blast, and he broke free of the charred remains of the minotaurs holding him. In an instant, he was on the other ifrit, his hands wrapping around the man's throat as flames engulfed them both.

"Betrayer!" the ifrit spat, his voice rasping as Zev's fire consumed him. "I will have my revenge."

"Who are you?" Zev demanded.

"I am Kintus," the ifrit snarled. "First and last-born son of Aulerci, adopted son of Taranis, and I will avenge my father and rid the world of your filth and lies!"

Nearby, Ryker dispatched the last minotaur with a vicious thrust of its own horn. She turned toward the fight, her sharp eyes narrowing. "Zev, I can see his magic!" she shouted. "He's half-djinn! He's not a full ifrit!"

Zev hesitated, his flames flickering. "He's mortal?" he asked, his voice cold and terrifying.

Ryker nodded. "You can kill him!"

"Together," I said, staggering to my feet and moving toward Zev. "We'll take him out. I'll channel my power into yours." I placed my hands on his back, the bond between us flaring to life as my fire merged with his.

Kintus screamed as our combined power overwhelmed him. His body convulsed, his flames faltering. "Taranis!" he roared, calling out to his god. "Aid me!"

But no divine help came. He was shit out of luck.

Kintus's flames began to die, but before we could finish him, a brilliant flash of light erupted nearby. A stunning woman with long, dark hair appeared in the clearing, her presence radiant and commanding. Her dark eyes were wide with desperation.

"Kah'ar," Zev said, his voice trembling.

"Za'fir," she cried out, stepping toward him. "Don't kill him."

"And why not?" Zev demanded, his flames still burning. "You used him to betray me! You tried to seal me away."

"No!" she said, her voice breaking. "He is my son. I saved you from him. I didn't know what he had planned. He used my phone to track you and brought you to Taak Island where he laid the trap. I found him before he could finish and sent you back. I saved you, Za'fir. I would never allow you to be bandished."

Her words rang sincerely, and something in her expression made me pause. "Why would you choose your brother over your own son?" I asked, my voice steady but curious.

Kah'ar's lips quivered. "Because Za'fir is also my son."

I froze. Holy shitballs, Batman. This was a mic drop I had not expected.

"I wasn't allowed to raise him as my own," Kah'ar continued, her voice shaking. "So I became his sister, his champion. Even when he betrayed me, I still loved him. I still love him."

Zev's flames dimmed, his rage giving way to confusion and pain. "This... Is this true?" he whispered.

"Yes," Kah'ar said, tears streaming down her face. "You have always been my greatest joy."

Kintus took advantage of Zev's weakening resolve. With a furious snarl, he yanked away from us and rolled across the pavement away from us. I thought he might be trying to escape, until he was back on his feet, body surging with energy as he lunged for Zev. In his hand was the bandish hex, the metal plate glowing.

"I love you, my son," Kah'ar whispered. She stepped in front of Kintus, wrapping her arms around him as he charged. "Remember me."

Before Kintus could react, she pressed her palm against the sigil and held it to his chest. His eyes widened in horror. "Mother!" he screamed as his body dissolved into smoke. Kah'ar's form shimmered, and she too began to fade.

A crystal bottle appeared between them, the swirling smoke of both mother and son drawn inside. The stopper sealed itself with a final, magical click, leaving the clearing eerily silent. Then the bottle disappeared.

Zev fell to his knees, in stunned silence. I knelt beside him, placing a hand on his shoulder.

"She loved you," I said softly.

He nodded, his eyes, lakes of fire. "She always did."

Around us, the forest was quiet. The gods had no more champions here.

Chapter Eighteen

WE RETURNED TO THE HOTEL AFTER RYKER called for a magical clean-up crew to take care of the bloody and charred mess at The Grand Treehouse Resort. I promised Biv I'd return the next day with her bounty, and then Veronica dropped us off at the hotel. Carver and Rowan were reunited, and they'd made a beeline for the suite without the fire damage to catch up on lost time. Zev and I said our good-nights to them and headed down the hall to Carver's old room to sleep in the smokey bed.

The night was quiet, except for the soft whir of the air conditioner. I held Zev close, his head resting on my chest as I ran my fingers through his dark hair in slow, soothing strokes. My heart ached for him. The weight of losing Kah'ar was too much for him to process. He'd trusted she wouldn't betray him, and his trust had been well-placed. She hadn't just been his sister—she was the mother he never knew and now never would. Her sacrifice spoke volumes about her love for him, but it also left a hole in his heart that hadn't been there before.

"I don't know how to feel," Zev murmured, his voice raw and unsteady. "She sacrificed her life to save me. She was my mother. I didn't even know."

I pressed a kiss to his temple. "You don't have to know how to feel," I said softly, tears cresting my eyes as I thought about my own mother. When she'd died, I went on a self-destructive binge of bad food, bad booze, and bad men. I'd acted out in ways that I never even told Iris about. Her death had wrecked me, so I'd finished the job. At least for a little while. "Grief is messy," I told him. "Let it be messy."

"I loved her," he said. "Even when I thought she hated me, I loved her."

"I know," I whispered, my chest tightening. "And she loved you. That's why she did what she did. She gave you your life back."

I held him tighter, willing myself to absorb his pain. My love for him swelled, fierce and consuming, as though my body couldn't contain it all. His pain was my pain, and I ached to take it from him. When holding him wasn't enough, I kissed him gently, offering him everything I could. We made love slowly, tenderly, until the sorrow gave way to something else—something raw and healing. In those moments, the pain ebbed away, replaced by waves of shared ecstasy that chased the hurt away, at least for a little while.

THE NEXT MORNING, Veronica drove me to Berryville to rent a car since mine was toast. The small town bustled with morning activity, but there was a lightness between us that felt like a new friendship.

As we pulled into the rental office, Veronica grinned at me. "I've been thinking," she said, her tone casual. "I'm going to head back to Illinois. I want to rejoin the Sister of the Bloom Coven."

My eyebrows shot up in surprise. "Really? What brought this on?"

She shrugged, her smile softening. "Being with you reminded me of how important family is. I miss mine. And... it's time to grow up, you know? I want to learn more and be more. Maybe even become someone my mom can brag about. Instead of someone she assumes is getting hexed."

I laughed. "You're already someone to brag about, Veronica."

Her eyes lit up at the compliment. "Well, maybe one day I'll have a hot djinn of my own."

I laughed harder, shaking my head. "I'll put in a good word with Zev. Maybe he has some single friends."

At the rental place, we shared a quick hug before parting ways. I drove to Walmart first, got me a new phone, and bought all the nuts with shells off their shelves. Afterward, I returned to Eureka Springs and hauled the motherload to Biv. The squirrel was flippin' delighted. Ovi and Doub rolled around in the nuts and threw them in the air like high rollers who had hit the jackpot. I thanked Biv for her help with a kiss and a pat on her furry head, then headed to the hotel to pick up the guys, the fresh start of the day lifting my spirits.

When I pulled into the yellow zone, I spotted Rowan, Carver, Ryker, and Zev waiting by the entrance with bags.

Carver greeted me with mock sternness. "You owe me seven thousand dollars."

I blinked. "For what?"

"For the antique bed you destroyed," he said, folding his arms dramatically.

Zev snorted, draping an arm around Carver's shoulders. "I'll pay it," he said with a grin. "Totally worth it."

I noticed Ryker didn't have a bag. "Where's your stuff?"

"I'm sticking around for a few days," she said.

"This wouldn't have something to do with a certain kitchen witch, would it?"

Ryker shrugged. "She mentioned she could use some help packing up."

Veronica had mention that she dabbled, and Ryker was stunning, so I couldn't blame Veronica for wanting to dabble in her direction. "You have fun with that." I grinned at my half-djinn friend, who'd come through for us again, then gave her a hug. "Thank you, Ryker. For everything."

"Call me anytime," she said. "You know how to throw a party."

I laughed. "I think I'm going to retire from my party days."

"Hah!" She shook her head. "Good luck with that. Until next time."

Ryker said her goodbyes to the guys, then headed toward the Grotto Coffee Shop.

As I threw my bag in the car trunk, I noticed Rowan and Carver holding hands. My brother's nervous eyes darted to me like he was bracing for a reaction. Silly man.

"Are you okay with this?" Rowan asked hesitantly, gesturing between him and Carver. "I mean, I know you're okay with it, but I mean, are you okay that I never told you?"

Without hesitation, I stepped forward and pulled them both into a hug. "Okay? I'm thrilled. I'm so happy you're happy, Ro. And you never have to worry about what anyone in the family will think. We love you, and we don't care if you're gay, straight, bi, or any letter you happen to be. You're you, and that's all that's important to me."

Rowan relaxed against me, the tension melting from his frame. "Thanks, Mare. That means a lot."

I pulled back, meeting his gaze. "Take your time telling the rest of the family. Or don't. No pressure. Just know I'm here for you whenever you're ready. It's your beautiful truth to share." I paused, letting the moment settle before grinning. "You do realize I was the first one Iris came out to as a true-craft witch. I've got a pretty good track record with keeping secrets."

We climbed into the car, Carver and Rowan in back, Zev and I up front. As the wheels hit the road, the heaviness of the last few days seemed to lift a little. The bad times were behind us, or the first time in what felt like forever, the future looked bright and sunny. I couldn't wait to find out what happened next.

THREE WEEKS LATER...

Since leaving Eureka Springs, my life had been like a fevered dream of happiness. Zev and I had settled into an easy rhythm. Our days and nights were filled with good conversation and fantastic sex. The passion between us could trigger a seismometer —it was off-the-charts volcanic. I hadn't realized I'd been craving this kind of happiness and peace until I'd experienced it with Zev. I'd put my witch studies on hold for now—just to enjoy life and savor a bit of time with the man I loved. No looming threats, no life-or-death stakes. Just us.

Tonight, we were heading to my father's house for a family dinner. He'd invited everyone, including my youngest sister, Rose, her husband, Don, and their energetic boys, Iris and her fella, Kier Quinn, and Iris's son Michael, who was now nineteen and deep in debate over whether to stick to his gap year or head to college in the fall. Rowan and Carver would be there too, and for the first time, they were out to the family as a couple. Even Dad was happy for them and seeing him so proud of Rowan made me proud to be his daughter.

Zev squeezed my hand as we walked up the front steps. This was his first big Everlee dinner.

Sure, he knew all my family, but this was his first time as a full-fledged member of the Everlee tribe. He fidgeted with the buttons on his blue Henley.

I smiled up at him. "Don't be nervous, and don't let Rose's boys rope you into a wrestling match. Last time, Don couldn't walk straight for three days."

"I think I'm in better shape than Don," Zev chuckled. "But noted."

Inside, the house was alive with conversation and laughter. Dad was in the kitchen, stirring something on the stove while Iris set the table with Michael. Rose and Don were in the living room with the boys. Rowan and Carver stood near the fireplace, holding hands as they talked to Dahlia about Rowan's latest antique find for his house.

Dad looked up as we entered, his face breaking into a wide grin. "There they are!" He held out his arms, and I hugged him. "The lovebirds," he said. "I wondered when you were going to come up for air."

"Daaad." At that moment, I was his little girl again, and that gave my heart wings.

Zev held out a bottle of wine he'd brought along. "Thought this might pair well with dinner."

"Perfect," Dad said, taking the bottle and pulling Zev into a one-armed hug. "You're a good man, Zev. Welcome to the madhouse."

"Thank you, Mr. Everlee," Zev said warmly.

"Mr. Everlee?" Dad chuckled. "Call me Randy. If you're making my daughter this happy, you're already family."

The evening felt like a dream. The room buzzed with warmth and laughter, and every so often, I'd glance at Rowan and Carver, grateful they'd found each other. The acceptance and love felt like everything I'd ever wanted for my family. It's funny how things work out sometimes.

At one point, I leaned into Zev's and whispered, "I am so freaking in love with you."

"And I you." His golden eyes softened as he looked down at me. "I'm yours, my love. Now and always."

Blushing, I excused myself and sashayed toward the bathroom. Everything about tonight felt perfect, and I couldn't help but marvel at how blessed I was. As I reached the bathroom mirror, I leaned closer to check the faint lines at the corners of my eyes.

"Smile lines," I murmured, grinning at my reflection. Because I hadn't stopped smiling since we'd returned to Southill Village.

I turned the faucet on, rinsing my hands in the cool water. As I reached to turn it off, steam began to rise from the faucet, curling upward until it clouded the mirror.

I froze, as the condensation spread across the glass.

Then, as though an invisible hand was swiping through the mist, words appeared, stark and deliberate:

Did you think I forgot about you? The hunt begins.

I stumbled back as the message disappeared. "Oh, crap," I muttered, my stomach twisting into a tight knot.

The warmth of the room suddenly felt oppressive. My perfect night, my perfect life was suddenly shattered like glass.

And that pissed me off to no end.

"Come on," I said out loud. "Come and get me."

Whoever this was, whatever they wanted from me, I would make sure they got a lot more Marigold Everlee than they bargained for. They would regret the day they ruined my Zen.

The End....for now.

FIND out who's hunting Marigold at the conclusion of this trilogy *Stand By Your Djinn*!

Stand By Your Djinn
(Destiny of a Middle-aged Witch Book 3)

I'm Marigold Everlee, a middle-aged eclectic witch who doesn't have to look for supernatural trouble because supernatural trouble finds me. Especially now that I have been bonded to a fiery ifrit in a way that has the entire djinn world quaking in their bottles.

My life takes a sizzling turn when a malevolent supernatural creature come after me, hell-bent on unraveling the secret to my bond with Zev. As the dark force closes in, I have to summon every ounce of my magical prowess to protect our bond and keep out of the creature's grasp. But with Zev's flames flickering and my own strength waning, the line between savior and captive blurs.

Will we burn brighter together, or will this infernal enemy snuff out our love for good? Hold tight, because in the Everlee family, survival is never just a spark—it's a full-blown inferno.

NEW TO THE GRIMOIRES UNIVERSE? Get **Earth Spells Are Easy** to see how it all began.

As a forty-three-year-old, newly divorced, single mom, I know two things for certain, starting over sucks, and magic

isn't real. At least that's what I thought. I mean, starting over really does stink, but when it comes to magic, I have to rethink everything.

I've spent the last year since my ex left me going through the motions. Get up. Work. Care for a grumpy teenager. Cook dinner. Go to bed. Wash. Rinse. Repeat.

Nothing changes... Until it does.

After bidding on a box of old books at an estate auction, I'm experiencing changes.

And I'm not talking about menopause.

My garden gnome Linda has come to life. No, really. Her name is Linda, and she never shuts up. A chonky cat with a few secrets of his own has adopted me. And a gorgeous professor of the occult tells me I'm a witch.

Right now, I'm not sure who's crazier—me, Linda or the hottie professor.

If this is my new reality, it's nature's cruel midlife trick. I'm learning fast that earth spells might be easy, but they aren't cheap. All magic exacts a toll, and if I don't master the elements, the elements will be the death of me.

Literally.

Praise for Renee George

"Grimoires of a Middle Aged Witch is my new favorite series! I want a gnome named Linda of my own. Trust me. Read the series. You will not regret a single delightfully hilarious and heartwarming moment.

~ *Robyn Peterman, NYT and USA Today Bestselling Author* of *Good to the Last Death series.*

"I love Renee's books, and recommend any of her series! They catch me right up and keep me turning those pages."

~*Yasmine Galenorn, New York Times Bestselling Author*

"Renee George has crafted a fantastic start to this magical midlife adventure. Pick up Earth Spells Are Easy today! You won't be disappointed."

~*Dakota Cassidy, USA Today Bestselling Author*

"I'm loving the Paranormal Women's Fiction genre! Renee George's humor shines when a woman of a certain age sniffs out the bad guy and saves her bestie. Funny, strong female friendships rule!"

-- Michelle M. Pillow, NYT & USAT Bestselling Author

About the Author

I am a USA Today Bestselling author who writes paranormal mysteries and romances because I love all things whodunit, Otherworldly, and weird. Also, I wish my pittie, the adorable Kona Princess Warrior and my two cats Ash and Simon could talk. Or at least be more like Scooby-Doo and help me unmask villains at the haunted house up the street.

When I'm not writing about mystery-solving werecougars or the adventures of a hapless psychic living among shapeshifters, I am preyed upon by stray kittens who end up living in my house because I can't say no to those sweet, furry faces. (Someone stop telling them where I live!)

I live in Mid-Missouri with my family and I spend my non-writing time doing really cool stuff...like watching TV and cleaning up dog poop

Follow Renee!
Bookbub
Renee's Rebel Readers FB Group
Newsletter